GUARDIANS

OF THE **WILD**

UNICORNS

To my sister Susan, with all my love, and many apologies for the roundabout incident. xx

Kelpies is an imprint of Floris Books
First published in 2019 by Floris Books. Second printing 2019
© 2019 Lindsay Littleson

This publisher acknowledges subsidy from
Creative Scotland towards the publication
of this volume

MIX
Paper from
responsible sources
FSC® C013056

 Also available as an eBook

British Library CIP data available
ISBN 978-178250-555-6
Printed in Great Britain by TJ International

GUARDIANS OF THE WILD UNICORNS

LINDSAY LITTLESON

Kelpies

1

Lewis

Rhona peered over the edge of the cliff, grinning like a gargoyle. Far below, Lewis dangled in his harness, legs kicking, frantic with fear.

"You were meant to hold on to the rocks!" she called, her voice choked with laughter. "You weren't supposed to let go!"

"It isn't funny," he muttered. "Shut up, shut up, shut up."

Terror was making his guts clench, his throat tighten. His palms were so clammy they slid on the rope. This was the polar opposite of funny.

He was making a fool of himself, as he'd known he would. His list of fails was getting longer. He was rubbish at rugby, clueless at kayaking, a failure at football and now, brand new to the list, abysmal at abseiling. And that was the edited version, not the complete list. Not even close.

The instructor on the ground was yelling instructions, but he might as well have been speaking in Mandarin, like Lewis's mother when she chatted on the phone to Grandpa in his Beijing flat. Lewis could only make out every fifth word, then or now.

He was too far up, a dizzying, terrifying distance from Earth. If his harness broke, he'd plummet head first onto rocks. He could imagine the sickening crack as his neck snapped on impact, his skull crushed, brains oozing from under the helmet, gloopy as frogspawn.

That was the one thing Lewis excelled at: imagining worst-case scenarios.

It was no struggle to picture his mother's face when she got the phone call telling her the tragic news; he could hear her breaking down, distraught, sobbing at his funeral. "My poor boy! He had his whole life ahead of him. I should never have let him go. Why was I so selfish?" A major downside of being dead would be his inability to answer back, to remind her that he'd told her many times that he didn't want to go on the trip, and she hadn't listened, that she'd never listened.

"Oi! Lewis! You look like ma granny's soap on a rope!"

The vision dissolved and Lewis was dragged back to real life, dangling from a cliff face, jagged rocks below, helpless as an upended beetle. Imagining his own funeral had been more fun.

"Belt up, Rhona. It's not funny." Lewis had been aiming for irritated, but instead his words flew out as squawks of panic. Rhona burst out laughing.

"You should see it from up here! It really is funny. It's bloomin' hysterical."

Scott leant over the cliff edge and waved a gloved hand. "Right, Lewis! No worries! We're bringing you down!"

The rope moved and Lewis was mortified to hear a whimper of terror that could only be his. Slowly, the rope started to descend and his body began to spin, like a hanged corpse. Lewis opened his eyes, saw jutting black rocks and squeezed them shut again. But the spinning rope was making him so dizzy he was scared he might spew, so he prised his eyes open and focused on the horizon: jagged mountains, a vast expanse of bleak moorland.

And then he saw it.

At first, it was a dark smudge, far in the distance. The smudge was moving fast, tracing a path across the moor, arcing like a shooting star across the sky. As it came nearer, he could see it was an animal: huge, broad-backed, long-legged.

Lewis blinked, unable to believe his eyes, which wasn't unreasonable: his eyesight was dodgy and his glasses were tucked inside his rucksack. Oblivious to the swinging rope, he kept staring; even Rhona's raucous voice faded into the background.

It couldn't be. Lewis blinked again, trying to clear his vision, remove what could only be a mirage.

Though that can't be right, can it? Mirages happen in deserts and there are no deserts in Scotland, it's too wet. Although on second thoughts, Eastgate's a desert. No cinema, no theatre, no museums. It doesn't even have a Costa. All you can do in Eastgate is get a haircut, buy booze or place a bet… Right, stop havering… Need to focus. There isn't anything weird going on. Nothing weird at all. Everything's fine.

But when he stopped blinking frantically and looked again, he could still see it. Across the moor galloped a huge dark beast, a heavily muscled horse with a gleaming, rippling black mane. The animal reared up, its hooves cutting the sky and its silken tail streaming like a banner. Its spiralled horn glinted in the sun.

Lewis blinked again. But the animal didn't vanish. He was still staring at a unicorn.

It has to be a dream. Or maybe I've died of fear. Maybe I've landed in a parallel universe, a Jurassic Park full of extinct creatures. That wouldn't be so bad. I've just humiliated myself in front of everyone. If I've landed in an alternative universe, I won't have to see any of those losers ever again.

Maybe I should just let go of the rope… but I don't want to be dead. Eleven's too young to die. There's stuff I really want to do, once the hell that is Eastgate is over. I'm going to visit my relatives in Bejing, learn to drive a Maserati, become a world-famous artist and get another dog, one that nobody will take away from me…

"Hey, guys. Keep the area clear, will you?" yelled Scott. "I need to bring Lewis down safely!"

It dawned on Lewis then that he couldn't possibly be dead. He was still hanging from the rope, still cringing with shame. When he looked towards the ground, he saw Flora Dixon sniggering and pointing upwards.

Lewis closed his eyes and kept them closed, tried to ignore his heaving stomach. Being sick over Flora again would be a VERY BAD THING. Once had been humiliating enough, but he tried to convince himself it didn't matter. He was basically dead to Flora already. His abseiling fail was just another clod of cold earth, dumped on top of his coffin. When his heels scraped against rock he wanted to weep with relief, but the nightmare wasn't over. By the time he'd struggled to unbuckle all the straps and buckles on his harness, Derek McIvor was scrambling down the cliff face, bawling "FREEDOM!"

Oh, great. Even Derek has made it down the mountain. I'm now officially wimpier than Derek the Dweeb. I'm the Wimp King.

Miss James, who taught infants and must have been bribed into coming on the Primary 7 residential, gave him a sympathetic smile. "Never mind! You gave it a really good try!"

9

He grimaced, unable to think of anything polite to say. He could imagine the shock on her face if he said what he was feeling: "Save that stuff for the little ones. Leave me alone."

For another endless, torturous hour, Lewis huddled beside a large rock, shivering, as clouds covered the sun, and freezing rain started to fall. Rhona had commented on the rock earlier, saying that it looked like Pikachu, and although he'd told her she was havering, he had to admit he could see a resemblance. Standing next to his favourite Pokémon didn't make him feel any happier about watching the rest of the class swing over the cliff edge and abseil fearlessly down.

Could we not have gone on this trip in June instead of April? There would have been less risk of losing my extremities to frostbite.

One by one the others reached the bottom and ran over to join the huddle. For a few minutes they leapt about, bouncy as wallabies, screaming with hysteria-tinged laughter. Then after a while, when the adrenaline wore off, they calmed down and started comparing abseiling techniques as if they were seasoned mountaineers, not a bunch of kids from the East End of Glasgow who'd never climbed anything higher than the stairs of a multi-storey flat before in their lives.

Miss James, full of that irritating infant-teacher fake enthusiasm, stood at the bottom of the cliff, taking photo after photo for the school website. "Oh, well done! Well done! Great job!"

I'm surprised she's not handing out 'Miss James says Good Effort!' stickers. And how many pictures does she need to take? It'll be like seeing it all again in real time. Please let there be no photographs of me dangling in that harness – or worse, video footage for YouTube. Oh heck, I'm going to go viral. Why didn't I just throw myself off the cliff and have done with it?

Mortified, and with no techniques to contribute, Lewis drifted apart from the group. He knelt, hunched over his rucksack, making pointless adjustments to the straps, while rain trickled down the back of his neck. Sometimes he'd straighten up and stare across the moor, searching for the unicorn. With his glasses on, his eyesight was near-average, and at one point he spotted a herd of red deer ambling uphill towards a distant pine wood. The stag was in the lead. He was taller and heavier than the hinds, with great branching antlers.

It could have been that stag I saw earlier. It must have been him. It's the only logical explanation. My eyesight must be getting worse. I'd better let Mum know, so she can make me an optician's appointment. She should have let me get contact lenses last time, then I wouldn't be half-blind.

When Lewis thought about his mother, he got a bitter taste in his mouth. This was officially the second-worst week of his life and it was totally his mum's fault.

"You need to go on this trip, Lewis," she'd said, waving the form, oblivious to his hunched shoulders and scowling face. "Maggie says her best childhood memories are of the P7 residential; she says it was terrific fun. Midnight feasts, having a laugh with her pals…"

"And if I go you won't have to organise childcare for five whole days," he'd muttered, forgetting that his mum's hearing was keener than Wolverine's. "You'll get to go to that conference, after all."

"That's unfair, Lewis," she'd sighed. "I've already told Maggie I can't go."

It might not have been fair, but it was accurate. No sooner had Mr Deacon prised the booking form from Lewis's reluctant fingers, his mum had been on the phone to her boss.

"Guess what, Maggie? I can make the conference after all! Where are you planning to stay? Can I get myself booked in too?"

So Mum and Maggie were staying at a posh hotel in Edinburgh. Lewis had googled it before he left and discovered that it had a heated swimming pool and a luxury spa. The Outdoor Centre had neither. Now, *that* was unfair.

When it was Rhona's turn to abseil, she hurtled down the mountainside at double-quick speed, whooping all the way down. Her round cheeks were flushed with triumph when she arrived at the bottom.

"That was amazin'! Did you see me?" she yelled at

nobody in particular. Lewis glanced at Flora, saw her roll her eyes. Anger surged through him.

She's got a mean streak as wide as the Clyde. I wish I'd thrown up on her after all. And I was higher up this time. The puke would have gone over her head instead of her shoes.

Rhona yanked off the helmet and harness, waved at the group and ran over to Lewis. "That was incredible! I thought I was goin' to wee myself when I went over that ledge. It's so high up!"

Lewis shrugged and continued to stare at a fascinating clump of lichen by his feet. He'd convinced himself that frostbite was setting in, that his toes were about to turn as black as burnt chipolatas and drop off, one by one. Even Rhona, his best pal in the world – let's face it, his only pal in the world – was getting on his nerves. She was enjoying herself, not missing home one bit, so he couldn't even whinge without her trying to talk him out of it and jolly him along. But he knew Rhona was used to him being quiet. She could talk enough for both of them.

"I bet it won't be so bad next time! Now that we know what we're doing! You just need to hold tight, Lewis, and use the belay thingy to control your speed. You'll be fine." She craned her neck upwards and waved her arms like wind turbines. "Can I go again, Scott?" she bawled. "And can Lewis have another go an' aw?"

Scott stood at the top of the cliff and waved down at

her; he seemed to have no fear of heights. When Lewis was up there he'd kept low and clutched at tufts of grass, convinced the cliff edge was about to break off, or that he was going to flip forward and fall.

"Light's starting to go. There isn't going to be time," said Scott.

"Aw, go on!"

"Shut up. I'm not going down that cliff again," Lewis hissed, appalled. "Specially not with you, you eejit. You were meant to be abseiling, not free-falling."

Rhona peered at him. "Don't get snarky. I just thought if we went together it wouldn't be as scary. You should have told Scott you don't like heights. It's nothing to be ashamed of, you know. I'm the same with snakes."

"Yeah, but heights are all over the place in Scotland. They're hard to avoid. Being scared of snakes is unlikely to be a big issue, is it? How many snakes have you seen outside the zoo?"

"None, yet, 'cept that big adder slithering up your trouser leg. Ha, made you look!"

"Grow up, Rhona."

"No way. That isn't happening. I'm the Lassie Who Never Grew Up. Like Peter Pan, but ginger and female."

She grinned at Lewis, and despite his black mood, he felt the corners of his mouth twitching.

"Oh wow, you actually cracked a smile! I thought your

face had forgotten how! Aw, if we had our phones you could have taken a selfie."

Lewis fished around in his brain for something to say, but his mind seemed to have been ambushed by unicorns. An enormous herd of unicorns was galloping around in his head, snorting, neighing, kicking their hooves. He felt his face flush, and he turned away from her, focused on hauling his rucksack onto his shoulders.

"Give over, will you?" he muttered.

One thing was for sure, he couldn't tell her that while he'd been swinging from that rope he'd imagined he'd seen a unicorn. She'd think he had lost his mind. He was already the odd one out at school, the solitary freak who always had his nose in a book. Now he was the freak who spotted unicorns. When he closed his eyes, he could see the unicorn again: powerful and magnificent, roaming free across the moor.

2

Rhona

Rhona considered telling Lewis he looked a total numpty, standing there with his eyes shut, but she didn't want to make a bad situation worse. She breathed in her surroundings instead and felt a shiver of joy at the sight of the darkening sky, the vast, empty moor, distant snow-capped mountains. There was so much space and freedom here. The thought of going home, back to the cramped, grotty flat, back to Mum, felt suddenly unbearable.

She focused on Scott instead, and whooped as he abseiled expertly down the cliff. "Gaun yoursel', big man!"

Lewis tsked at her, but she tried not to mind. Embarrassment was making him crabbit. He'd get over himself in no time.

The whole group, minus Lewis, cheered Scott on as he clambered towards the ground. Miss James took more photos and made more enthusiastic comments. Rhona smiled fondly.

"Miss James is dead nice, isn't she?" she said. "I loved her to bits when I was in P1."

Lewis didn't respond. At least he'd opened his eyes, but he wasn't looking at her, just staring into the distance, a troubled look on his face. It was as though he'd been turned to stone, like the wee hairy guy in the movie *The Lion, the Witch and the Wardrobe*. For a moment Rhona had an eerie feeling that something terrible had happened to Lewis when he'd been dangling from that rock face, but she shook the feeling off. Lewis would've have told her. They were best mates. Then she flushed, remembering she hadn't told *him* everything.

She found herself gazing in the same direction, scanning the horizon. She nudged Lewis, trying to spark some life back into him. "Are you OK, Lewis? You look a bit dazed. You didn't bang your heid during the Great Abseiling Disaster, did you?"

Lewis rubbed at his eyes, blinked at her. "No, I didn't, worse luck. I'm just fed up and frozen." He gestured towards the others. Max, the other instructor from the Outdoor Centre, was gathering up the gear, half-heartedly assisted by Mr Deacon. Mr Deacon's nose was red at the tip, his woolly hat drenched. "Mr Deacon looks miserable too. I bet he's wishing himself back in the Primary 7 classroom.

Teaching fractions to Derek has to be marginally less grim than this."

Rhona grinned. "Naw, he's loving this," she said. "No jotters to mark and he can use the instructors to help keep the class in order. He even gets time off during the day. The residential must be a breeze for him compared to school."

"You think?" Lewis shrugged. He didn't look convinced.

But then Lewis didn't know Mr Deacon like Rhona did. He had no idea how kind the teacher could be, and Rhona wasn't about to tell. Her problems were her own business, no one else's.

Scott reached the bottom of the cliff. He strode over, beaming and waving, and whipped off his helmet. Rhona gulped. Scott was like someone off the telly. He was *so* good-looking, boy-band handsome, with sun-bleached blond hair, tanned skin and twinkly blue eyes. He glowed with health and fitness, a poster boy for the Australian Tourist Board.

"That was pretty cool, wasn't it, guys!" he said. "Brilliant work today. Bet you're all mega proud of yourselves."

When Scott smiled, Rhona found herself grinning back.

"Stop it. You're like a brainwashed zombie," muttered Lewis.

"You're just jealous, cos he's gorgeous, an' you're no.'"

"At least I'm not a big fake."

"That was incredible!" gasped Flora, grabbing Scott's

arm. "I thought I'd never be able to do it. But I did! I was a total star!"

Scott smiled and gave her a thumbs up, but his eyebrows raised a fraction. Rhona bet he found Flora really, really annoying but was too polite to say. She'd tell Flora to her face if she didn't stop winding up Lewis.

"You've all been total stars!" Scott beamed. "Every single one of you."

"One of us hasn't been a total star," Lewis sighed. "One of us has been utter rubbish."

Flora's mouth opened, ready to give her opinion. Rhona gave her a very hard stare. Flora's lips clamped shut.

Scott pointed at the teetering pile of gear. "Let's get ourselves organised and back to the Centre for tucker. And don't forget it's the ping-pong derby, followed by storytelling round the campfire!"

"Yay! Tomorrow night will be karaoke and a quiz with amazing prizes, and Thursday's our disco!" Max grinned. "I bet you can't wait!"

Rhona glanced at Lewis. She bet that every single one of those activities would be his idea of hell on earth. He'd clearly heard Max, and if he hadn't been in such a stinking mood she'd have burst out laughing at his appalled expression.

"All this socialising is doing my head in," he grumbled. "When am I supposed to get peace to read?"

Rhona didn't even try and answer that one. "I'm starving. Hope there's loads of chips," she said cheerily, hoisting her borrowed rucksack onto her shoulders. "An' apple pie with custard, or rhubarb crumble and ice cream for afters." She gave Lewis a sharp poke in the ribs. He was doing that weird staring thing again. "Stay away from the custard. You've got a face on you that would sour milk."

Lewis drew his eyes away from the mountain, gave her a rueful grin. "You wouldn't be so flaming cheery if you'd just humiliated yourself in public."

Rhona smiled back, glad he'd returned to planet Earth. "Lewis, do you see anybody who's bothered?"

"Well, if they're not bothered, I am. I hate it here, Rhona. I want to go home."

"You can't though, can you? You said your mum's away working. Mr Deacon won't let you go home to an empty house, so there's no use you pretending to be ill."

"Today was the pits. I preferred day one, when I spent hours underwater in an upside-down kayak."

Rhona tried to swallow her rising irritation. "Lewis, it was seconds. You should have held your breath instead of gulping in water."

"I did hold my breath! But I'm not a flaming goldfish. I was actually drowning. It was horrible."

Rhona sighed. The kayaking had been amazing. They'd seen an osprey skimming the still water, a huge fish dangling from its talons. Lewis might be hating every moment, but this was the best week of her life, and he was starting to spoil things. Since they'd arrived, it was as if he'd got stuck in a bog, sucked down into misery, and she wasn't able to reach him, no matter how hard she tried.

The two teachers, the rest of the P7 pupils and Max and Scott were getting further away, dotted and clumped in groups along the path as they headed back to the Outdoor Education Centre building.

"Come on, Lewis. We need to go." Rhona nudged his arm with a heavily padded elbow. The white quilted jacket kept her warm as toast, but she thought it made her look like a wee fat snowman. A wee, fat, grubby snowman… The jacket had been dragged by Mr Deacon from the bottom of the lost property box when he'd spotted Rhona getting on the coach dressed in a thin cagoule and jeans. At least nobody had accused her of nicking it… yet.

Lewis didn't move, so she tried more food-based persuasion.

"Imagine your plate piled with steaming-hot fish fingers and chips with tomato sauce. Imagine being too late and me eating all of yours."

"I'll be ready in a second."

"Hurry up! They're all ahead of us. We'll be last served. My stomach's thinking my throat's cut."

21

"I'm coming. I just need to pull up my socks. My left heel's got a massive blister."

"I've got blisters on my blisters, Lewis. But I'm no' moaning for Scotland."

"No, you're not moaning, that's for sure. It's as though you've morphed into a flaming cheerleader."

Rhona grinned, quite enjoying the idea. "Give us an L! Give us an E! Give us a W!"

"If you're trying to cheer me up, you're doing a lousy job."

She waved imaginary pompoms around, bouncing up and down in front of him.

"Quit it. You're bugging me." Lewis kicked a clod of wet earth. Slurry mud splattered on Rhona's white jacket.

"Ha! Is that so, big man? How's this for annoying?" Rhona flicked her foot just as Lewis stepped forward – and tripped him up. Not just a basic trip… a massive face-first splat.

Rhona gasped, knowing she'd gone too far. As Lewis lay there, sprawled in the mud, her heart started to bang against her ribs, afraid she'd just killed their friendship stone dead. There was a terrible silence, broken only by a distant buzzard keening above them.

3

Lewis

Mud oozed up Lewis's nose. Icy rain trickled down the back of his neck.

Just when I thought my day couldn't get any worse, my best pal shoves me in the mud. Bet that bloomin' buzzard swoops down now and tries to peck out my eyes.

Rage burned a hole in his brain. "Look what you've done! I'm soaked!" He stumbled to his feet, fists flailing. He couldn't see, blinded by mud and rain, but one of his fists landed, drove through something soft and squishy, crunched against bone.

"Ow! Ya flamin' eejit!"

Lewis's anger fizzled and died. He wiped at his face with his sleeve to clear the mud from his eyes.

"Rhona? Are you OK? Did I hit you? I didn't mean—"

She clutched her arm. Was that rain or tears streaming down her face?

"That hurt. Get lost," she spat, and she stormed off towards the Centre, leaving Lewis alone on the moor, lost in despair.

At first he could see Rhona's white jacket bobbing along, glowing like the moon. But then the little white blob disappeared, as if a cloud had covered it. It didn't matter how hard he stared; Rhona was gone, vanished into the evening mist that swirled over the moorland. He sat down on a rock and let loose a torrent of swear words, most of them learned from Rhona.

She started it. She deliberately tripped me. I could have hit my head and been killed. Then she'd be sorry.

He shook his head, like a dog with fleas, trying to rid himself of the guilt, but he remembered clenching his fists, swinging his arms, the burning rage he'd felt.

Maybe, after all, despite everything, he was turning out like his dad. But he couldn't be, surely, because it had been so long since he'd seen his father he could hardly remember what he looked like. Tall, he thought, though maybe that's because he'd been so small in comparison. Thinning fair hair and glasses. Lewis had inherited his mother's black hair, but his dad's short-sightedness. His dad had worked in a bank, until he got made redundant, but like Lewis, he'd loved art and history. Their favourite place in the world had been Kelvingrove Art Gallery. They'd used to go on Saturdays, to marvel at the dinosaur fossils and the trays of crystals and the Egyptian mummies. But then Dad had changed and the art gallery visits had stopped. Lewis shuddered, remembering his father's smell on that terrible night, toothpaste masking stale alcohol and of his voice, desperate, slurred, as he ran after the car, banging on the window.

"Lewis! You know your old dad. I wouldn't hurt a fly! It was a mistake! I didn't mean any of it…"

A huge sob broke from Lewis's throat, and then the tears started falling and wouldn't stop. He slumped, head on knees, and stayed there on the moor as the sky darkened and the rain teemed down.

As darkness fell, the temperature plummeted. Thick grey mist swirled across the moorland, making the place seem as eerie as a zombie graveyard. The temperature had to be below zero, he reckoned, especially if the wind chill factor was taken into account. He'd packed light, too light: just his lunch and a Mars Bar. And he'd eaten both hours ago. No matches, no torch, no survival blanket. If he stayed out here on the moor, he was doomed.

Then the shivering started.

Right, that's it. I'm in trouble now. Hypothermia's setting in. People die of hypothermia.

He didn't know how long it took, and even if he'd been allowed to bring his phone on this trip, he couldn't google information out here in the Internet Dead Zone. He brushed rain out of his eyes, spoke aloud to break the terrifying silence.

"What the heck do I do now? I don't know what to do…"

There was a frayed, panicky edge to his voice that was even scarier than silence.

Calm down for a start, you eejit.

Staying out in this bleak, foggy moorland was stupid. He knew he should head back. He knew which direction to go. Well, he was fairly sure he did.

If the mist clears, I should be able to see the lights of the Centre. But if I wait too long they might turn them off. Then I'll be totally lost. I'll end up wandering round like that poor guy, what was his name? The one who got stuck in a canyon for weeks and had to cut off his own arm. He was trapped and he was dying of thirst. He drank his own pee in the end. It was gross. There's no way I'm doing that.

Lewis got up, stretched out his arms, like a blind man feeling his way, and stumbled a couple of steps. But his left foot sank into wet, cloying mud. He tried to lift it out. It wouldn't budge. Overwhelmed by panic, afraid he *was* actually trapped and would be swallowed up, he struggled frantically, his foot sinking deeper into the slurry peat bog.

"Help! Help me! I'm stuck!"

Thick mist snaked round his voice and choked it.

There's no one here to help, you saddo. You need to do this yourself.

Lewis took a deep, gulping breath, grabbed his leg, and tugged with all his strength. Nothing happened. His foot stayed stuck, and now his other foot seemed to be sinking too. He'd definitely seem a film like this... by the time the rescuers got to the victim, only his hat had been visible. The man had been sucked down, choked to death by mud.

He took another deep breath and, once his breathing slowed, he tried again, channelling Princess Leia strangling Jabba the Hutt. He took hold of his calf and pulled. His boot came free with a disgusting squelch and he staggered backwards. Heart banging against his ribs, he limped back to the rock. He crouched beside it, tugged his hood over his face and tried to come up with a better plan: a plan that involved him getting home to his own bed, his own home.

There's a station at Arichdour, about three miles south. If I walk there I could buy a ticket to Glasgow, sneak back to the flat, break in through the kitchen window, and when Mum gets home I'll pretend I'm just back. I could drop hints about smoking or drugs or bullying on the trip. No, maybe not. She'd only phone the school and Mr Deacon would call me a liar. I could tell her I'm never going to pass any exams and need to move to a school that isn't scraping the bottom of the league tables. Mr Deacon can't argue that one.

It wasn't that he was desperate to go back to Bellwood Academy. His life had changed so much in the last four years that he doubted he'd have anything left in common with his old friends. Sam messaged him occasionally, but he always seemed to be on his way out to rugby practice. While Lewis enjoyed watching the Six Nations on television, he was hopeless at playing it himself and wasn't keen to improve his skills, either. He'd read about rugby players who died of broken necks or ended up paralysed. It was too dangerous to even be called a sport. It was all football at Eastgate, but he wasn't keen on football either.

Rain dripped off the end of his hood, splashed onto his numb, frostbitten nose.

He needed to move, but if he fell into another peat bog, his corpse might not be discovered for thousands of years, like Tollund Man. Mr Deacon had talked about Tollund Man during last term's topic on prehistoric times and they'd found out all the grisly facts about how he'd been killed. Even all the scientific stuff about how they'd worked out his age from the state of his bones and teeth had been interesting. Now it just felt scary. Lewis didn't want to be a mummified corpse. He didn't want scientists musing over his Scottish and Chinese parents or tutting over the filling in his back tooth and deciding he'd eaten too many Haribo in his short lifetime. He wanted to go home.

Lewis got up and squelched along for what seemed like

endless hours when he stopped dead, struggling to take in what he was seeing right in front of him: it was the rock that reminded Rhona of Pikachu. His stomach clenched. Hot tears gathered in his eyes. He'd been travelling in a circle. He was back where he'd started, at the foot of the abseiling cliff.

The rain was falling so hard that the world looked blurry, out of focus, but the mist had shifted, become torn and threadbare. Mountains, dark and misshapen, loomed above him. The wind had dropped and darkness was creeping closer. Even if he could try again to squelch to Arichdour, he had no idea of the train times. There was nothing else for it. He'd have to find his way to the Centre. Horrible as the prospect was, he'd have to face them after all, even Rhona, or die of exposure on this hillside. Thinking of Rhona was painful, like stubbing a toe or standing on Lego. He couldn't imagine dealing with high school without Rhona; she was always around – taking his side, mocking his fears, making everything bearable. And now she'd never speak to him again, and it was his own fault.

Collapsing against the rock, shivering, he sank down, oblivious to the wet ground. His brain felt fuddled. All he wanted to do was lie in the shelter of the rock, curl up into a ball and go to sleep. He felt too warm and wondered if he should take off his jacket.

It took a long moment to register that something was coming, heading towards him across the moor. At first he thought it must be Scott in his pick-up. His head swam with relief. The instructors had realised there was a pupil missing and were coming to the rescue. But then it dawned on him that the sound was wrong: it wasn't the rumbling of a vehicle, more a deep, rhythmic drumming.

It was as if the earth was shaking. He could feel the tremor through the soles of his feet, thrumming through the rock he was leaning against. It was a low, thumping sound, like the thudding of hooves. The sound got louder and louder, impossible to ignore. A terrible thought grew in his mind.

It's the unicorn. It's coming to get me.

He threw back his hood and peered through the drizzle. It must be a hallucination. But hallucination or not, it was the unicorn and it was coming straight towards him.

Almost invisible in the mist, dark grey against purplish heather, the huge beast galloped alone. As it thundered towards Lewis, he could see it more clearly: muscled flanks, flowing black mane. Steam billowed from its quivering nostrils and its spiralled horn gleamed like steel. The unicorn was a huge, frightening beast, but it wasn't on the attack – it was terrified.

Lewis felt the animal's fear, heard the loud drumming of its heart, shared its panic. It wasn't coming for him.

The unicorn was the prey. Somebody was hunting it down, and the beast was crazy with fear and confusion.

Lewis ignored the part of his brain that was yelling at him to hide. He stood up and moved from the shelter of the rock and spoke clearly, urgently, desperate to soothe the panicking animal.

"It'll be OK. I'll help you, I promise. Don't be afraid."

The last thing Lewis saw was the horn, long and dagger-sharp, as the animal lowered its great head and charged.

4

Lewis

"I thought you were deid!"

Lewis's eyes were closed, and his head was spinning, but he could hear Rhona's voice, loud and clear.

Rhona's here. She's come back for me...

"Why did you stay out there all by yourself when it was getting dark? You're scared of the dark, you big lummox! I've been up to high doh! What if you'd died? What would I have done then, you selfish git?"

She ranted on for a bit longer while he lay there, luxuriating in the warmth of the room, the heaviness of the covers on his body, the softness of the pillow under his head. He was in bed, and he was safe, and he couldn't have been injured because he didn't seem to be in any pain. And he was definitely not dead, because he could hear Rhona's voice. She might have been raging, but at least she was speaking to him.

When Lewis opened his eyes, Rhona's face swam into focus. She looked upset, teary-eyed and pale, rather than angry.

"I'm sorry." he whispered. "I'm so sorry."

Rhona's eyes widened. Then she smiled, two dimples appearing in her cheeks. "Aye, I'll not shove you in any more bogs and you keep your flailing hands at peace. But why didn't you follow me home? I thought you were huffing in the boys' dorm when you didn't come for your dinner. It wasn't till Mr Deacon did one of his head counts that I realised you were still out there. Mr Deacon was raging with *me*, which was hardly fair."

Lewis couldn't trust himself to speak, so he lay still, staring at the ceiling, hot tears stinging his eyes. Rhona squeezed his hand. He knew it was meant to be reassuring, rather than a crush, but it hurt all the same. Rhona never knew her own strength.

"I'm glad you're not deid, Lewis. I thought you were a goner."

Did he nearly die? It was all a terrifying blur. Closing his eyes, he could see himself, huddled against the Pikachu rock, shivering with cold, panic exploding in his chest as he listened to the sound of hooves thudding on grass...

The unicorn... Somebody was hunting the unicorn. I promised...

33

Lewis opened his eyes and the vision vanished, replaced by Rhona's red-rimmed eyes, her crooked smile.

"How did I get back here?" His voice was weak, a cracked whisper.

"Scott and Mr Deacon went out looking for you. Scott says you were shaking all over. You gave them a real fright. They got the out-of-hours GP to call in, but he said you were faking."

"He said what?"

"I'm joking, Lewis. He said you were 'mildly hypothermic' and you'll be right as rain. Though he also said it's lucky it isn't winter, or you'd have been dead for sure."

The door opened and Scott peeped his head round. He smiled at Lewis, but his eyes had lost their twinkle and his voice was stern. "You gave us a right scare, mate. What were you thinking of, lagging behind like that? We've phoned your mum. She was hacked off that you didn't follow orders, but glad you're safe. She asked if she should come and collect you. I said I was going to leave that up to you. You can tell me now or wait until morning. You're going nowhere tonight, as the doc's coming back in to see you first thing."

Shame burned Lewis's cheeks. His first instinct was to ask Scott to tell his mum to come. The thought of going home was so appealing that it was almost impossible to turn his back on the prospect. But he could picture the white-lipped fury on his mum's face, the endless, silent drive home. And if he went home, he'd be abandoning Rhona. She'd been looking forward to this trip for months, talked about it non-stop. She was his best friend. He couldn't do it to her.

"Can you phone my mum back and tell her I'm sorry?" he said. "And I don't need to be collected. I'll be home on the bus with everyone else on Friday."

Rhona squeezed his hand again, crushing his index finger. "I'm glad you're no' goin' home and I'm glad you're no' deid. Sleep well, Lewis. At least you'll not have to listen to Derek snottering and snoring all night. I'm off out to the campfire."

When they'd left the room, Lewis lay in the darkness, his mind racing.

What happened to me out there on the moor? Maybe bad memories got tangled in my head and my brain turned them into something solid. Maybe I just went crazy, alone in the cold and the dark.

Shivering, he pulled the covers over his head and tried to sleep, but every time he closed his eyes the unicorn came charging towards him, mad with fear, about to pierce his flesh with its horn…

Giving up on the possibility of sleep, he flung the covers off and looked at the time. Only an hour had ticked by since Rhona had left. It was going to be a long, restless night. Maybe some fresh air would help.

He walked to the window and pulled it open. The night air rushed in, cooling the stuffy room. Smells of wood smoke and sizzling sausages drifted in with it. His stomach rumbled. He wasn't sorry he'd missed the ping pong, but the campfire stories might, after all, have been fun.

As he got back into bed, he jumped, because outside, in a voice so loud it carried across the field, someone had just mentioned unicorns. He lay still and listened.

"Folktales about unicorns abound, but the one most often told around these parts is the story of Whindfall Forest…"

The man's voice was hypnotic, mesmerising, and Lewis closed his eyes, picturing the story. The legend was thrilling, he thought, as he drifted off to sleep, but the reality had been beyond words.

5

Rhona

As Rhona closed the door of Lewis's room, she felt the tension seep from her body. Her shoulders sagged with relief and tears trickled unchecked down her cheeks.

"I'm ragin' at him," she mumbled. "But I'm so glad he's OK."

"Come on, Rhona," said Scott, his voice brisk. "You've missed your dinner, and all this evening's games. I don't want you missing the campfire too. There are sausages, hot chocolate and toasted marshmallows. How does that sound?"

She was starving, so it sounded amazing, though she was gutted that Lewis was going to miss out. As she followed Scott outside, she breathed in the cold, pine-scented night air, the warm smell of smoke. The wind had whisked the rainclouds away and it was a calm, dark night, so much darker than in Glasgow. Even the stars were brighter, sparkling like diamonds on black velvet.

Everyone was huddling round a blazing campfire, singing daft songs. They'd finished their sausages, but Mr Deacon had kept two for her, and Miss James handed her a cup of hot chocolate. She'd joined in the songs, eaten her blackened sausages, drunk the lukewarm liquid and was sitting beside Derek, toasting gooey marshmallows, when Scott called for quiet.

"Listen up, guys, and say hiya to Alex McAllister. He's a ranger at the Langcroft Estate, and he has kindly agreed to come along tonight and tell you some old Scottish stories. Isn't that right, Alex?"

Alex McAllister was at the other side of the campfire and Rhona could only make out a tall, shadowy figure.

"Thanks, Scott. Hi, all. Yes, I work at Langcroft, but I've actually lived on the estate for most my life. My parents died when I was small, and my sister and I were brought up by our uncle, who owns the estate. Can you imagine growing up surrounded by these mountains and glens? From a very young age I became fascinated by the local wildlife, and I've just finished a degree in Animal Biology at Stirling."

Derek let out a noisy yawn and Rhona poked him in the ribs. Alex was still talking, his loud, clear voice ringing in the dark.

"This is a very special area, and one that's steeped in stories. The one I'm going to tell you was told to me by my Uncle Donald when I was around your age. It's about unicorns."

Rhona pulled a marshmallow from the fire. It was sticky and delicious. She popped another onto a sharpened stick and held it close to the glowing embers as she listened.

"Folktales about unicorns abound, but the one most often told around these parts is the story of Whindfall Forest. Whindfall lies only five miles from here and according to legend is the last sanctuary of Scotland's unicorns."

"Can we go and see them?" shrieked Flora. "Mr Deacon, can we go and see the unicorns?"

Mr Deacon's voice was icy. "Hush, Flora, don't interrupt. And it's a story. Unicorns aren't real."

For a second, the fire lit Alex's face and Rhona saw him raise an eyebrow, as if Mr Deacon had said something foolish. Then he carried on.

"The story goes that long, long ago there were great herds of unicorns in Scotland. People respected their power and magic and left them in peace. But in the Middle Ages, as trade with other countries became more and more important, greed won over respect and humanity. Unicorn horns were stunning, much prized objects, and the traders started rumours that they held incredible healing powers. So the unicorns were hunted for their horns, much as rhinoceros are today, and, like the rhino, the once great unicorn herds became almost extinct and were scattered, leaderless."

The logs crackled, and red-hot sparks danced in the embers. Rhona's marshmallow burned to a crisp as she pictured the unicorns galloping across the moors, constantly in fear of their lives, lost, refugees in a country that had once been theirs.

"A stallion named Dubhar took charge. 'Dubhar' means 'dark shadow' in Gaelic. He rounded the frightened survivors into one herd, a hundred strong, and led them north to safety. They travelled only by night and faced a thousand dangers: fleeing hunters and their slavering hounds, fighting off attacks by packs of starving wolves, fording swollen rivers and struggling through snowy mountain passes, until at last they reached a great forest. As they trotted through the ancient trees, past glittering streams and deep, clear pools, the unicorns knew they'd found the perfect sanctuary.

"Dubhar called on Beira, the Queen of Winter, deer herder and mountain maker, and asked her to cast a spell that would keep them safe for ever, in beautiful Whindfall Forest.

"She agreed, on one terrible condition. Dubhar accepted her terms.

"So Beira crashed her magic hammer down to put a protective charm round Whindfall Forest, and cast a curse: nobody who enters the forest intending to capture or harm a unicorn will live to see winter. The unicorns at last had the safe haven they needed."

He stopped speaking, and except for the crackling flames, there was silence, broken by a hearty laugh from Mr Deacon.

"Well, Flora, I guess we'll not be visiting Whindfall Forest. Just in case the unicorns think we're there to cause trouble!"

But something was bothering Rhona. "What was Beira's condition?"

There was a heavy silence. Then Alex said, "Dubhar agreed to sacrifice himself. Beira turned him to stone because she wanted him to decorate her mountain throne. Now statues of Dubhar are all over Scotland, in every city and town market square. Look carefully and you'll see them. Stone unicorns are everywhere, but, according to legend, the only living unicorns left in the world are in Whindfall Forest."

He paused, and then stood up and stretched, a gangly silhouette.

"Well, you've been wonderful listeners. Thank you. Good night."

Scott stood up too. "Thanks so much, Alex. Yup! Time for bed, guys! I'll make sure this fire's safely out."

Rhona poked at the fire with her stick. Wisps of smoke floated from its embers and formed a shadowy shape. Rhona gasped, and Derek turned.

But the smoke had already drifted upwards into the night sky, and the unicorn shape she'd seen in it had vanished.

6

Lewis

Lewis had drifted off to sleep dreaming of Dubhar and his herd thundering across the moor, heading to the safety of the forest. But his dream became a nightmare when Dubhar turned and charged towards him, steam billowing like smoke from his flaring nostrils. The unicorn lowered his huge head, preparing to charge, and Lewis ran for his life and fell into a peat bog, up to his neck. Terror rose in his throat and he tried to scream, but he was turning to stone and his scream was silent. He tried to move his arm and hit something hard, sent it flying. The crash woke him.

Nothing was broken: he'd knocked a book off the table. All was well. He lay back on the pillow, breathing slowly. His sheet was twisted round his legs, and the blanket was lying in a crumpled heap on the floor, kicked off during his nightmare. When he put his hand on his forehead it was clammy with sweat, and he felt shivery, as if he was coming down with a fever. But when the doctor came, he left again within minutes, after listening to Lewis's chest and checking his blood pressure.

"He says you're in splendid health, but probably best to rest today," said Scott. "So I'm afraid you'll miss the gorge walk. Highlight of the trip as well. Mr Deacon has kindly said he'll stay behind in the Centre. He has your end-of-term reports to write, you'll be pleased to hear. Your mate Rhona is going to stay too and keep you company, so we're sorted. I'll bring you in some brekkie!"

Lewis was angry with himself because Rhona was going to miss the gorge walk. He heard the crunch of boots on gravel, and his classmates' voices drifting in through the window.

"What actually is a gorge walk, Scott?" asked Flora. "It sounds really scary!"

"You know perfectly well what a gorge walk is, Flora," snapped Miss James, sounding much less bouncy than she had yesterday. "It was thoroughly explained during the pre-trip talk."

"It's a walk through a gorge, basically, so you're going to get wet!" called Scott. "It'll be a real challenge, especially after all this rain!"

"Why's everyone wearing wellies?"

Trust Derek McIvor to ask a stupid question.

"Because you'll be walking through water, and some of it will be deep." Scott's voice sounded a little strained, as if his reserves of patience were beginning to run dry. "Derek, what have you got on your feet, mate? Go back and get your boots!"

"But my boots are soaking. I went up to my ankles in mud yesterday. Will my trainers not do?"

Lewis waited until the bus rumbled off, then tugged open the curtains. Sun streamed into the room. Outside, the scenery was breathtakingly beautiful, the sky bright blue. The moorland, burnished copper in the sunlight, was backed by jagged mountains, still snow-capped in late spring. He pushed the window further open, breathed in the fresh air. It was so quiet and calm. The tightness in his chest began to ease.

He jumped when the door was flung open and Rhona bounded in.

"Oops. I should have chapped. You could have been in the scud, but luckily you aren't. What are we going to do all day? Will we play Scabby Queen?"

They played cards for a while, but Rhona was a blatant cheat as always, so it didn't go well. While Lewis was very relieved not to be taking part in the gorge walk, guilt nagged at him because Rhona was missing it. She didn't seem at all bothered, but she was an expert at keeping her feelings hidden.

They didn't see Mr Deacon. He stayed in his room all morning, though Rhona raised her eyebrows when Lewis said he'd be working on their end-of-term reports.

"He'll be having a lie-in. He must be shattered, cos of the carry-on with you, and then Jay Fergusson spewing up all over his bed. At least Jay didn't sick up all over people the way you did. That was the funniest thing ever."

"Thanks for dredging that up, pal. It was four years ago, you know. Do you not think it's time to forgive and forget?"

Rhona grinned, eyes twinkling. "How could I forget The Day You Sicked Up in School? It was the day we became best pals."

"I'm not sure it happened that exact day. You weren't that chuffed when I puked over your shoes."

But it was true enough. If Lewis hadn't vomited in an art lesson during his first week at Eastgate Primary, he might never have become best friends with Rhona. When he'd arrived, looking completely wrong in his Bellwood cap, shorts and grey knee socks, Rhona had barely registered his existence. At the end of the first day, he'd pleaded with his mum to take him back to Bellwood. She'd pointed out that some of the Eastgate pupils were refugees from war-torn countries and must feel a lot more displaced than him, but it hadn't helped. Back then, all he could see was that everyone else seemed to have friends.

He'd been miserable and isolated, but his sick splattering on Rhona's socks had changed everything. It earned him the nickname Spewy Lewy for a while too, but that hadn't been Rhona's doing. Flora had thought up the name; even aged seven she'd known how to hurt.

While the other kids had shrieked in disgust as vile-smelling carroty sick spewed from Lewis's mouth and splashed over their masterpieces, Rhona had stayed calm. She'd wiped up the mess on her socks with a paper towel, ignored her wrecked painting, and focused on Lewis, standing shuddering in his plastic apron.

"That was boggin'," she'd said, head cocked like a robin's as she gave her diagnosis. "Your face is green as Shrek's, so you must have a bug. I'll get Miss McKay."

"Look what he did!" Flora Dixon's face had screwed up, and Lewis could still remember how ugly she'd looked, her neat little features distorted with rage. "My picture's wasted! There's sick on my shoes! I'm telling my mum!"

"Shut your trap, Flora!" snapped Rhona, shoving her hard. "He can't help being sick, and your painting was rubbish anyway."

Lewis had been sent home that afternoon, but when he'd returned the next morning, still feeling awful, Rhona had come to see him in the library corner, and had actually sat still for twenty minutes and listened while he'd read a chapter of *Harry Potter and the Philosopher's*

Stone aloud. He'd brought the book from home and had been keen to impress, reading without stumbling, even on 'mysterious'. Lewis remembered that he'd given Hagrid a funny, growly voice.

Rhona had been impressed: impressed enough to decide that Lewis would make an excellent replacement for Kayleigh Rutherford, who had been dumped as best pal after failing to invite Rhona to her seventh birthday.

She's been there for me ever since. And friends don't keep secrets from each other, do they? But what will she say if I tell her I saw a unicorn last night? Will she believe me or will she think I've lost my mind?

He decided he needed to try. "Can we move the subject away from vomit, please? I want to talk to you about last night."

Rhona put her cards down on the table and leaned back, a wary look in her eyes. Lewis chewed on his lip, unsure how to begin.

7

Rhona

Rhona could tell Lewis was anxious, and she could sense his reluctance to talk about what had happened out there on the moor. *Spit it out and get it over with,* she thought.

"First, I'm sorry I upset you," he said. "I wasn't thinking straight. I thought I'd hurt your arm, that you'd never speak to me again. I was afraid—"

Rhona shrugged. "I told you. We're even. Stop stressing." There was something else. She could tell. His face was ash pale. "I'm no' surprised you were scared, out there in the dark," she said. "I'd have been weein' myself." There was a short, strained silence, so she tried again. "Did you not think you were going to get savaged by a wildcat or chewed to bits by a wolf?"

Lewis shuffled the cards, seeming reluctant to meet her

eyes. "There aren't any wolves left in the wild. And wildcats aren't much bigger than ordinary cats. Anyway, wolves and wildcats avoid humans. They're not dangerous." His hands were trembling.

"Mr Deacon always says that if we talk about stuff that's worrying us, it drags the worries into the light, makes them shrivel up." Rhona didn't add that she always assured Mr Deacon that she had no worries to share, and that everything was fine, honest.

"You'll think I'm daft." Lewis spoke so quietly that she could hardly make out the words.

"Lewis, you're my best pal. Daft or not, I'll be on your side, whatever."

"I did think I saw something weird out there," he mumbled. "It must have been a mirage or something."

Rhona couldn't help it. Her eyebrows shot up. "A mirage? I wouldn't have thought so. You weren't crossing the flamin' Kalahari!"

"Yeah, OK. Mirage might be the wrong word. I don't know if it was a hallucination... a vision... an evil omen. But I saw a creature out on the moor. A really weird creature."

Rhona put her hand over Lewis's. She was really worried now. *Could he have concussion? Hypothermia?*

"Lewis, are you sure you're feeling OK? Forget what I said last night. You're not selfish... You were upset, and you weren't thinking straight… It's just that… you're my best pal, and—"

"Rhona, stop. I feel fine. I'm just trying to tell you what I saw. I'm not saying it was real. It was dark and I was scared and cold. It was terrifying, to be honest."

Rhona tried out the sympathetic smile she usually reserved for Primary 1 kids who'd fallen over in the playground. She was trying not to show how worried she was.

"So what did you think you saw?" she asked. "Was it a bird? Because there are some weird-looking birds up here and it could have been one of them. Black grouse and ptarmigans and capercaillies and such like. Birds you don't ever see in Glasgow. And they make some odd noises, Scott says."

"Jeez, Rhona. Do you think I'd describe meeting a strange bird as terrifying? I'm not a total wimp." He took a deep breath. "I'm pretty sure I saw a unicorn."

For once in her life, Rhona found herself stuck for words. She opened and shut her mouth, gasping like a landed fish, before deciding Lewis had to be having her on. "Good one! You nearly had me there. Did you have your window open last night? Did you hear the story that guy was telling?"

"I heard the story, but, Rhona, I promise I'm not joking. I thought I'd seen a unicorn earlier, in the distance when

I was abseiling, but when I was out on the moor, I saw it again—"

Rhona took her hand away, picked at her fingernails. She could no longer look him in the eye. *Should I call the doctor? Get Mr Deacon?*

A deep flush crept up Lewis's neck. But he kept talking. "I'm not joking, Rhona. I saw a unicorn. It was coming towards me, head down, twisted horn sharp as a spear. I thought at first I was going to get gored. It was the scariest thing ever."

Rhona looked up at him and nodded. She kept her voice quiet, trying to make him see sense. "Yeah, but you didn't see it, did you? You were hallucinating. Folk with hypothermia hallucinate. Sometimes they think they're boilin' and they take all their clothes off and freeze to death. You're lucky you just saw unicorns."

"I only saw one," he protested. "Not multiple unicorns. I wasn't that far gone."

"And it was charging at you?"

"It was blowing through its nostrils, like horses do when they're agitated. I thought it was angry at first, but it was afraid. It was really frightened, Rhona. Crazy with fear."

Rhona shook her head. He was totally havering now. "Doesn't sound like a unicorn to me."

"Oh, yeah? Unicorn expert, are you?"

"Kayleigh used to read all those *Rainbow Fairy* books."

Rhona spoke kindly, channelling Miss James. "Unicorns are gentle. They have big eyelashes, twirly rainbow horns and they let fairies ride on their backs." But as she spoke, she began to doubt herself. The unicorns in Alex's story weren't gentle. Their magic seemed much deeper and darker.

Lewis's face twisted with anger. "Fairies? Who mentioned ruddy fairies? I wasn't in flamin' Disneyland. There was a terrified unicorn stampeding across the moor. I saw it, and you know what? I don't care if you believe me or not."

He walked to the window and stared out. Rhona followed him, tried to put her arm round his shoulder, but he shook it off.

"OK, so you saw a wild animal." Rhona spoke slowly, trying to pick her way towards a logical explanation. "Are you sure it wasn't an escaped rhinoceros? There's a safari park near Stirling."

He spun round. "It wasn't a rhinoceros. Do you think I'm stupid? It was a unicorn."

Rhona saw Lewis's blush deepen. Surely he must realise how mad his story sounded?

"At least, it was a big dark-grey stallion with a horn on its head. It was definitely not a rhino. I know what a bloomin' rhino looks like."

"OK, but unicorns aren't dark, Lewis. Unicorns are snowy white. Everyone knows that."

But is that true? she wondered, remembering Alex's words. *A stallion named Dubhar, meaning 'dark shadow'. No, the colour wasn't the point. Alex was telling a story. He said so himself. Unicorns aren't real.*

"You can stop now." Lewis rubbed at his face with his hands. "I bow to your superior knowledge of unicorns, gained via second-hand information from kids' stories. I give up… admit defeat… concede… capitulate."

"Least I'm not a walking thesaurus."

Rhona pulled on her jacket. She'd loved Alex's story last night. She didn't *want* to disbelieve Lewis. But unicorns didn't exist. She needed to help him realise that. She'd prove it to herself too.

"Let's go for a walk. You're dead pale. The fresh air will do you good."

"Shouldn't we ask Mr Deacon? He'll freak if he comes out his room and we're not here."

Rhona shook her head. If Lewis didn't start talking sense soon, she'd tell Mr Deacon. He'd know what to do. But she was hoping desperately that it wouldn't come to that. "We can leave a note. Say we'll be back in half an hour. Bet he doesn't even clock that we've gone. Come on, Lewis. I'm going stir-crazy in here and I really think you need some time out."

While Rhona scribbled a note, Lewis pulled on his jacket and Timberlands. Rhona noticed that they were filthy, as if he'd been wading in mud. Maybe he'd tumbled out there in the dark and banged his head. That would explain all this unicorn stuff. There had to be a logical explanation.

They left by the main door. It was chilly outside, but the air felt pure and fresh, a zillion miles from the diesel fumes of Glasgow, and Rhona breathed it in, clearing her lungs. They walked along the track, then headed off into a damp wilderness of grass and heather. The peaks of the mountains were lost in cloud.

They headed downhill towards the loch. It was so peaceful and quiet. Lewis seemed calmer; his pale cheeks scoured red by the cold. He stood by Rhona at the lochside, as she flicked her wrist and sent the stone in her palm flying. It bounced off the smooth surface of the water – once, twice, three times – before it sank.

"How do you do that?" he asked her. "Any time I try, the stone plops underwater and refuses to resurface, or I miss the water completely. I should add it to my list of fails: 'seriously inept at skimming stones'."

"Stone skimming isn't that useful. At least you can read. I'm rubbish at it." Saying that aloud hurt more than she'd imagined, but Lewis didn't even seem to have heard her.

"I saw it," he said suddenly, his tone mutinous. "I saw a unicorn on the moor. You don't need to believe me."

"OK then, let's go and find your unicorn!" Rhona started walking up the hill.

8

Lewis

As he followed Rhona, a memory from last night flickered.

It'll be OK. I'll help you, I promise. Don't be afraid.

Why had he said that? What had been going on in his head? Why had he acted so weird, so completely out of character? Maybe he *had* been hypothermic, imagining he was some kind of superhero.

Halfway up, Rhona was sitting on a rock, waiting for him. "Glad you're not on a gorge walk?" she asked.

Lewis sat down beside her, felt the wind scud against his cheeks and whip his long dark hair into tangles. His mum would say that the tangles served him right and he ought to get it cut, but Lewis liked it long, and it was his hair, not hers.

"I'm a hundred per cent glad," he admitted. "I've already disappointed the instructors and Mum and made myself look a loser in front of everyone. The last thing I need is to topple into a gorge and get rescued by air ambulance. But I'm sorry you're missing out. You've taken to this outdoor stuff much better than I have."

Rhona didn't even bother to politely disagree with him. She nodded, her eyes sparkling. "It's amazing. I've never done anything more physically challenging than catching a bus to Buchanan Street. Now I've swung down cliffs like Tarzan, climbed mountains like Mulan, paddled a canoe like Pocahontas. I've had a brilliant time."

"You watch way too much Disney. And it was a kayak, actually, not a canoe."

"Whatever it was, it was great. Just being up here in the Highlands is great."

"There are warmer places." Lewis tugged at the zip of his jacket, so it covered the lower part of his face. "It's Baltic up here."

"Well, get up off your bahookie. Exercise will soon warm you up."

They kept walking until they reached the cliff face, scene of Lewis's abseiling fail. He put the binoculars to his eyes so they clinked against his glasses. Scanning his surroundings, he had to admit it: the Highlands were incredible. They were awesome.

But there were no unicorns. Not a single solitary specimen.

"OK, so it's a unicorn-free zone here", he admitted, and he could see the relief on Rhona's face. "I must have completely lost the plot last night. Let's go back and see if we can talk the catering staff into giving us some lunch."

They found a different route, heading in the rough direction of the Centre, following the path of a small stream that cut its way through dark-brown peat and soggy sedge grass. At one point the ground had caved in, leaving a deep pit. They walked carefully around it, hoping the ground wouldn't give way beneath their feet.

"Scott says these holes can be deadly in winter," said Lewis. "Imagine going for a walk in the snow and dropping into a deep hole. How freaky would that be?"

Rhona didn't answer.

She'd stopped a short distance away, head bent, staring down at something. Lewis strained his eyes to see what she was looking at: a large, misshapen heap, its colour blending into the dark, wet ground.

High up in the air, a buzzard keened. Lewis felt every muscle in his body tighten. The chill in his legs spread upwards towards his chest, a cold wave of dread.

"Lewis, what *is* that?" Rhona's voice sounded tight, strained.

His feet were frozen to the ground. He couldn't move, didn't want to see what was making Rhona's voice sound so peculiar, so afraid.

"Please, Lewis."

Heart banging against his ribs, he walked towards her and gazed straight down at the dark, long-limbed heap crumpled in the pit.

Rhona caught hold of his arm. "What's going on, Lewis? What's happening?"

Pulling out of her grasp, he backed away, acid rising in his throat, sick with shock and horror. He'd known what it was immediately, of course he had. The colour, the muscled body were all too familiar.

They were looking at the unicorn, and it was dead.

9

Lewis

The animal was lying on its left side, legs sprawled at awkward angles, muscled flanks splattered with mud. Blood trickled from a gaping hole in its neck, dripped from the animal's mane in stringy rivulets and formed a dark-red pool on the ground.

"It's been shot," said Lewis, keeping his voice low, knowing he was stating the obvious but trying to get the fact clear in his head. "It must have been shot as it ran, and fallen in here as it tried to get away."

However afraid he'd been of the unicorn when it was charging towards him, seeing it lying dead in a damp, muddy hole was horrific. All that power and beauty had been obliterated.

"Who would do such a terrible thing?" Rhona's eyes were wide, her face as white as her jacket. "You weren't hallucinating," she whispered. "I thought you were havering, but you weren't. And now it's dead. We need to tell someone, Lewis. The police, Mr Deacon…"

"Yes, killing a unicorn has to be illegal!" he agreed.

"Well, I don't know if it's illegal exactly. It's no' as if they're an endangered species like white rhinos or Sumatran tigers."

"What do you mean they're not endangered? They're meant to be extinct, aren't they? But they're not. At least they weren't…" Tears welled in his eyes and he brushed them away with his sleeve. "Do you think this might have been the last unicorn on earth?"

"Lewis, they're no' endangered. They're no' extinct. They never existed."

"Um, I'll think you'll find they did. There's one right there."

"But unicorns aren't real." Her voice sounded uncertain, which wasn't surprising. "They're like dragons, or kelpies…"

"Rhona, you're talking rubbish! They're not like dragons. Unicorns must have lived here once. They're Scotland's national animal."

"Don't be a numpty! Who told you that?"

"It's true." He clung to the fact with the same desperation he'd clung to the kayak the other day. "It was an article about Scotland in one of the magazines in the common room. Scotland's national animal is definitely a unicorn."

"Are you sure? Why would we have picked a mythical creature as a national animal? That's crazy."

"Well, it would be if the unicorn *was* a mythical creature, but it's clearly not, is it, stupid? As I already pointed out, there's one lying right there."

Lewis scrambled over the wide ribbon of sedge grass and clambered into the pit, ignoring the trickling water, the slimy mud. He knelt by the unicorn's body, stroked its tangled, sodden mane.

"I'm sorry, he whispered, tears dribbling down his cheeks. "It wasn't OK. I didn't help you. I'm so sorry."

10

Rhona

She was going to puke, she was sure of it. At first glance, she'd thought she'd found the body of a grey horse, tall as the massive Clydesdales the polis rode at Parkhead football ground, but slimmer built, and with peculiar cloven hooves. But then she'd seen the horn. Long, spiralled, as iridescent as the stone in her mother's opal ring; the ring Mum said was unlucky and refused to wear any more. This poor beast hadn't had any luck at all. It was a horrible sight, blood congealing on its neck and its muscled legs twisted.

"I don't understand what's goin' on, Lewis, but we need to get out of here."

At that moment Rhona heard a noise behind her. A Land Rover rumbled across the moor, bouncing over rocks and squelching through mud.

She gasped. "Hide!"

"Where?"

She looked round, heart thudding. If she'd been asked, she wouldn't have been able to explain why she thought they were in danger. She just felt it, the way she could sense how Mum's day was going as soon as she entered the house.

Lewis pointed upwards at the wide verge of green sedge round the hole.

They ran over and ducked under the overhanging grass. Then Rhona noticed a tunnel, round as a pipe. Water trickled from it, leaving the rocks green and slimy. Muttering swear words, she wriggled inside. Lewis squeezed in beside her. It felt horribly claustrophobic.

Rhona's jacket was so puffy that she could scarcely move. Not that she wanted to go any further back into a pitch-black, possibly rat-infested tunnel.

"We weren't trespassing," Lewis said aloud. "We've every right to be on the moor."

Rhona gave him a poke in the ribs. "Shut up and listen. They're here."

The Land Rover's engine died. A car door slammed, then another. Rhona heard a female voice, young and cold.

"It can't have got far. We should have come across it by now. I'm pretty sure I clipped it."

Someone swore.

"Aw, no. It's right there, Ailsa. Look, it's missed its footing in the dark and come a cropper, poor beast. We should have come earlier."

Rhona shivered. She recognised that voice. She was sure of it.

"I was busy, bro, upping security. But I'm sure it's only a flesh wound. You go down and have a look."

Rhona gulped. Her heart raced as she heard someone scrambling down into the pit, just a metre or two from where she and Lewis crouched.

There was a long, terrible silence. When the man finally spoke, his voice was thick, as if he was holding back tears.

"Oh my God, Ailsa. What have you done?"

Above them, the sedge grass shivered. A booted foot swung right in front of them. Rhona gripped Lewis's hand, convinced they were about to be discovered. There was a thud, and a dark shadow fell across the tiny cave, then a squelch of boots, as the young woman walked over to look at the animal she'd murdered.

"It was an accident," she said, her voice icily calm. "The beast was heading straight for the base of the cliff; I was just trying to scare it by sending a bullet whistling past its ear. I didn't shoot it in cold blood."

The male voice rose, his anger boiling over. "Why the heck didn't you use a tranquilliser dart? Look what you've done!"

"You know that one was vicious! What was I meant to

do? Let it gore me, like it tried to before? Tranquillisers take time to work."

"He isn't… He *wasn't* vicious. He was only trying to defend his herd."

"*His* herd? It's *my* herd!" Ailsa spat the words. "What do you know about anything anyway? You swanned off to university and left me and Uncle Donald to take care of everything. Langcroft is broke, bro. The breeding programme is going to save us."

There was a tense silence, broken by Ailsa's bitter voice.

"While you were off skiving, I was risking my life stalking ruddy unicorns. Do you know how hard it is to capture one unicorn, let alone sixteen? It's impossible in the forest; they're too well camouflaged. I had to wait outside Whindfall, sometimes for weeks, until they ventured out. That was no joke – you know how cold it gets in winter. I nearly lost my fingers to frostbite. I've been tossed in a river." Her voice rose. "That one almost gored me in the leg!"

"You should have left them alone."

She gave a joyless laugh. "I can't believe how ungrateful you are. Anyway, have you got any better ideas about how to make money?"

Another silence fell.

"Langcroft needs the unicorns." Bitterness soured her

voice. "You might be older, but you're brainless. I can't believe you're going to inherit Langcroft when I'm the one who's putting all the work into keeping it afloat."

"I didn't ask Uncle Donald to make me his heir, Ailsa ..." The man sighed. "Anyway, you have to tell him what's happened."

"No way," snapped Ailsa. "I'll just say I've looked everywhere but can't find the ruddy animal. Anything could have happened. Maybe it got lost, or fell into a loch."

"There's no chance of keeping this a secret. I mean, somebody else might have seen you. There are people all over the place: climbers, ramblers, school kids on residentials."

Ailsa sighed impatiently. "Why do you think I let the animal roam all afternoon? The moor was like a kids' playground yesterday. I had to wait until they all headed back. Trust me: there was definitely no one about last night."

"That's what you think, you bampot." Rhona's whisper echoed round the narrow space and she gasped, horrified by the noise she'd made. But outside the conversation carried on.

"And even if one of those wee brats filmed it and stuck it on YouTube, who would believe it? People would think it was a hoax. Unicorns don't exist, remember?" Ailsa's laugh was chilly. "Mind you, a horse with a glued-on horn is still an animal. People are so pathetically sentimental, they'd be less bothered if I shot a person."

The man gasped. "This really isn't funny, Ailsa, though I don't know why I'm surprised. You've always had a mean streak. Don't think I've forgotten what you did to poor Thumper."

"I still don't see why you got a pet and I didn't," she said airily. "I set your stupid rabbit free – it's not my fault a dog ate him."

The air twanged with tension. A jagged rock was digging into Rhona's back. The air was stale, the smell sulphurous.

"I still think you should go and see Uncle Donald and tell him what happened. Losing the stallion is going to wreck all his plans for a unicorn breeding programme."

Unicorn... Rhona finally remembered where she'd heard that voice before. She whispered in Lewis's ear. "*His* name's Alex McAllister. The storyteller from last night."

Lewis put a finger to his lips. Ailsa was speaking again, her voice icy.

"You don't get it, do you? We're not telling Uncle Donald the stallion's dead."

"Give me one good reason why not."

Ailsa's voice was stone-cold. "Because I'm taking its horn."

"What? You can't do that!"

"What do you think we should do with it then? Donate

it to charity? Unicorn horns are worth money – a *lot* of money. More than elephant tusks or rhino horns. Imagine what beautiful objects craftsmen will be able to make with them…"

Alex snorted. "Nobody will ever believe they're real. It's a crazy plan."

"It's been the plan all along, you dope. Remember last summer, when I went on safari to Africa? I wasn't taking photos of giraffes and ruddy wildebeest, I was meeting traders. I'll be able to sell the horns, alright, if I have DNA evidence that they come from an unknown species."

"Come on, Ailsa, talk sense." Alex's tone was mocking. "Even if you have a piece of paper to back you up, who's going to believe that it's a real unicorn horn? It'll never work."

"It doesn't matter. People will convince themselves the horn is real, if they want to believe it badly enough. Just like you and Uncle Donald have convinced yourselves these creatures have magic powers."

"But they do." Alex spoke quietly, but with complete conviction.

Ailsa scoffed. "If everyone else is as gullible as you, I'll be a millionaire in no time. The fact that the horns *are* real is just a bonus."

Rhona crouched against the damp rock, feeling sick.

Her brain filled with images she'd glimpsed on television: heaps of tusks, white as bone, long as spears; muddied elephant corpses buzzing with flies; tiny orphaned calves; blank-eyed poachers with guns slung over their shoulders. When terrible stuff like that came on the news, Mum tended to flick channels, back to the safety of celebrity quiz shows or cooking programmes, where ugly, tragic real life wasn't allowed to intrude. And now animal poaching had come here, to this beautiful Highland moor. It was going on right in front of them and they were helpless to stop it.

Alex was speaking, his voice trembling with disgust. "So let me get this clear. Uncle Donald told me this was a conservation programme, to boost the unicorns' numbers. Are you telling me it's a cover for a trade in horns?"

"Uncle Donald thinks we're planning a conservation centre for unicorns, but he's an idiot. I'm running it and I've got other plans."

"Ailsa, you can't be serious…"

"I'm deadly serious. Maybe you didn't notice while you were off partying at uni, but Langcroft is in deep trouble. The estate costs a fortune to run and Uncle Donald's broke. That's why we've had to let visitors in." She gave a bitter laugh. "You might not care, but I do. Langcroft's my home. *Mine.* I won't lose it because you and Uncle Donald can't face up to reality."

"But unicorn numbers are tiny. These are the only ones left in the whole world! You can't take their horns—"

"This is what's happening, Alex: we're going to breed the unicorns and we're going to make money from their horns. Losing the stallion is a setback, but we've still got thirteen mares – one of them pregnant already – and two young colts. They'll replace the stallion in the long term. Think of it as a unicorn farm. People breed alpacas, don't they?"

"It isn't the same," said Alex. Rhona thought he sounded close to tears again. "Not at all. You don't hurt an alpaca when you shear it. For all you know, hacking the horn off a live unicorn might kill it. Uncle Donald will never let you do this, he loves unicorns! We both do, since—"

Ailsa's voice snapped like a trap. "Not again. I'm sick of hearing about how brave wee Alex and kind Uncle Donald went on a camping trip together and rescued a unicorn from a peat bog. Blah boring blah."

Alex groaned. "Let it go, will you? Listen, I won't be part of this. I won't hurt any unicorns."

Rhona heard a scrabbling sound, boots slithering on mud.

"Alex, where are you going? You'd better not be leaving me alone with this… situation."

"Watch me. I've had it with you. I can't believe we're actually related."

There was a loud click. Rhona's breath caught in her throat. Beside her, Lewis gulped.

"Put the gun down. Stop behaving like an idiot, Ailsa." Alex sounded more irritated than afraid, but Ailsa's reply was chilling.

"I'm not joking, Alex. I'll shoot you, just like I shot this stupid beast."

"You'd never get away with it," There was anger in Alex's voice, and a tremor of fear. "Uncle Donald will know you did it."

"Lots of poachers around, bro. Accidents happen."

Outside, silence fell. Rhona could hear the drip of water, steady as a clock's tick. Then Alex spoke again.

"Put that blasted thing away. I'll help you get rid of the evidence, but I'm not going to do anything while there's a gun pointing at my head."

Rhona tightened her grip on Lewis's hand. His palms were sticky with sweat, his body rigid. His breathing was raspy and seemed so loud in the confined space that Rhona was afraid they'd be overheard.

"Thanks, bro!" Ailsa's voice was bright, as if nothing had happened. It made Rhona shiver. "Let's go back and get a harness or we'll never lift this beast."

"There's a harness and a hoist in the stables," said Alex, sounding defeated.

"And a hacksaw."

"A hacksaw?"

"Weren't you listening? The value's in the horn."

For endless minutes, Rhona and Lewis huddled, stiff and cramped, waiting until the Land Rover trundled off.

"We need to get out of here." Rhona half-pushed Lewis towards the entrance and then tried to follow, feeling a flutter of panic when her jacket got wedged tight. Lewis helped tug her free, but then all his adrenaline seemed to seep away. His knees buckled and his legs wobbled. She sat him down on a rock and went over to pay her respects to the unicorn.

Surely there's something I can do for it, she thought, *something to show that its death is mourned.*

As she wiped away tears, her hand brushed against the chain round her neck. *Of course…*

"Rhona, we need to go. We need to be well away before they come back," said Lewis.

Carefully, reverently, Rhona ran her hand through the unicorn's silken mane. "I'm so sorry," she whispered, tears streaming down her cheeks.

11

Lewis

Rhona flung open the door of the Outdoor Centre and both of them toppled inside.

"Woah!" Mr Deacon glowered at them, putting his coffee cup down on the table. "What on earth are you two playing at?" He pointed an accusing finger at Lewis. "This note said you'd be back in half an hour! You've been gone for twice that. I was about to come and look for you."

Lewis wanted to spill the whole story. This was too serious for two eleven year olds to deal with by themselves. They needed to pass the buck to a responsible adult. But he was struggling to get his own head round what had happened. How could he expect someone else to believe him, particularly if that someone was Mr Deacon? They weren't exactly on good terms. He'd go as far as to say the teacher actively disliked him. Deacon was always picking on him, trying to make him do stuff he didn't want to do, like work in groups or play team sports.

In last term's report Mr Deacon had written that Lewis needed to 'develop his interpersonal skills'. Mum had laughed and said that, loosely translated, he meant Lewis was the class grump. Lewis had been pretty offended by the whole thing. It wasn't against the law to prefer working on your own, was it?

But this was serious, deadly serious. And this wasn't about him.

"We found a dead unicorn," he said, trying to keep his voice from shaking. "We need you to call the police."

Mr Deacon raised his eyes to the ceiling. "Oh, very funny. Ha blooming ha. Dead unicorn indeed. You've been a liability on this trip, lad. I thought you'd gone and got lost again. And Rhona, you're supposed to be keeping an eye on him."

"He isn't joking, Mr D." Rhona pulled off her jacket. Her cheeks glowed, scarlet as traffic lights. "We only went for a dauner. But then we found a deid unicorn. Honest!"

Mr Deacon's eyes softened. "Oh, I get what's happened," he said, using a kindly tone Lewis wasn't used to hearing. "That wasn't a dead unicorn you saw. It would be a red stag. I'm afraid there's always the risk of seeing an animal being shot up here in the Highlands. The gamekeepers have regular culls of the deer. I'm sorry you two had to see that, I really am."

Lewis shook his head. "Mr Deacon, it wasn't a stag. It was—"

"It *was* a stag, Lewis. Let's stop this right now, eh?" Mr Deacon raised a warning hand, then picked up his cup and took a swig. "You're back safely, and that's the main thing."

There was a firm note in his voice, and Lewis got the message loud and clear.

A door swung open and one of the catering staff bustled in, carrying a tray. She gestured at Mr Deacon with a jutting elbow.

"I saw the two lassies coming in and thought you might like some lunch. The others took most of the ham, but I've made some cheese sandwiches."

Mr Deacon beamed. "Thanks, Janet. You're a star."

Rhona growled, and gestured at Lewis, who felt his face flush.

Leave it, Rhona.

"We're no' two lassies. We're one girl and one boy. You need to get yoursel' some specs."

Janet peered at Lewis, her eyes narrowed, as if she thought he was trying to trick her. "You should get yourself a haircut, lad. How on earth was I to know?"

Mr Deacon sighed. "There was no need to be rude,

Rhona. The last thing we need is grumpy catering staff. They might run off and leave us to starve."

Rhona grabbed a cheese sandwich from the plate and took a large bite. "You should have said something yoursel' then, shouldn't you?"

"Yes, you're right. I should. I'm sorry, Lewis."

Lewis gawped. If he'd spoken to Mr Deacon like that, he'd have got the hairdrier treatment and double detention. "It's OK. It doesn't bother me. I know who I am," he said.

Mr Deacon grinned at him and gestured at the plate. "Come on, you two, let's eat outside. It's too glorious a day to be stuck indoors. And Lewis must be starving after all last night's drama."

They headed outside and sat on a bench by the main entrance, munching and chatting away.

The sandwiches were delicious, cheese and tangy pickle in thick slices of white bread. There were grapes too, and glasses of apple juice.

Lewis was half-listening to Rhona and Mr Deacon's chat when he heard a car engine, loud and throaty, as if the exhaust was shot. Looking up, he saw a beaten-up Land Rover, bumping over the rutted road, heading straight towards them.

Rhona's face was bright with panic.

Mr Deacon shaded his eyes so he could check out

the driver. "Someone's in a hurry. This isn't the M74, pal."

The Land Rover swerved to the right, braked too fast and slid to a halt by the bench. A girl swung down from the vehicle. Lewis guessed she was about nineteen. She was tall and angular, dressed in a tweed jacket, jeans and boots. Her hair was ash-blonde, cropped short.

Lewis noticed that Rhona's hands were trembling as she zipped her parka up over the lower half of her face and pulled her hood down.

"Stay calm," he murmured. "Maybe it isn't her. And even if it is, she's never seen us before in her life."

"Good afternoon!" called the girl, striding towards them. "I'm Ailsa McAllister, gamekeeper at the Langcroft Estate. Are you staying here at the Outdoor Centre?"

Mr Deacon ran a hand through his thinning hair and tried to smooth it down, but the wind was too strong and greying strands waved in the air like octopus tentacles. "Yes, we are," gabbled Mr Deacon. "We're on a school trip; we've come all the way from the East End of Glasgow. It's an amazing experience for our pupils. Some of them have never been out of the city before. We're having a fabulous few days, aren't we, kids?"

Lewis and Rhona nodded in agreement, though Rhona kept her face half hidden, chin tucked into her parka. Lewis was about to whisper that her disguise was pure rubbish, but when he glanced at her face he could see fear in her eyes.

"Oh, yes. You must be from the group my brother Alex visited to do a storytelling session." Ailsa smiled at Mr Deacon.

She *was* very beautiful, in a chilly, elegant, fashion-model sort of way. Her lipstick was a slash of red, her eyebrows immaculate curves, her eyes cat-like, but Lewis thought her smile looked as friendly as a she-wolf baring her teeth. Even her voice seemed fake friendly, so unlike the way she'd spoken to her brother.

"Yes, the kids really enjoyed the storytelling. It was good of your brother to come along," said Mr Deacon, beaming. "I've heard great things about the Langcroft Estate's outreach programme. You do impressive work for young people with your team-building activities."

"That's my brother for you, always super-keen to help. And Uncle Donald loves to encourage children from inner-city areas to come along and explore the facilities – for free." Ailsa smiled again, but it didn't reach her eyes. "We've always got hordes of children running around. Well, we'll get a break tomorrow – a group has cancelled."

Mr Deacon's eyebrows shot up. "Oh really? We tried to get a slot at Langcroft when we booked this trip, but you were full up… Is there any chance we could come along tomorrow morning instead?"

Ailsa's fixed smile didn't slip, but Lewis saw annoyance flash in her eyes.

"Of course, how lovely. We'll look forward to that very much."

She can't think of a reason to say no, Lewis thought, *so she's not as smart as she likes to think. And she obviously doesn't have a clue we've seen the unicorn.* The tension in his shoulders started to ease.

"By the way," said Ailsa. "I found something that might belong to one of your pupils."

She was addressing Mr Deacon, but her amber eyes swivelled between Rhona and Lewis.

She rummaged in her pocket, held out one hand. A St Christopher's medallion glinted in her gloved palm. Lewis glanced at Rhona.

Rhona bit her lip, but said nothing.

"That's yours, isn't it, Rhona?" said Mr Deacon, completely oblivious to the tense atmosphere. "I seem to remember asking you many times not to wear that medallion in the gym."

Rhona swallowed, held out a shaky palm. "I must have dropped it yesterday when we were abseiling," she said. "Thanks for bringing it back. My mum gave it to me when I was small. It's… it's supposed to bring me luck when I'm travelling."

"Rhona's always losing stuff." Lewis tried to keep his

voice casual, but even to him, his tone sounded fake.

Ailsa turned towards him and stared, unblinking, as if she was trying to extract information from his brain.

"Well, I'm delighted to be able to return it!" Ailsa turned to Mr Deacon and held out her right hand. "It has been a pleasure to meet you and your delightful pupils. Please do come tomorrow. I'll get Alex to organise some outdoor activities for you all!"

She got into the Land Rover and drove off, gears crunching.

Mr Deacon rubbed his hands together. "Well, isn't that terrific! Right, we'd better head inside so I can carry on with these reports.

"Would it be alright if we stayed out here for a while?" Lewis racked his brain for an excuse. "Um… I was thinking I could start work on my personal research project. The capercaillie is on the RSPB's red list. That means it's in real danger of extinction. Scott says he thinks he heard one in the pine wood behind the Centre. I've got my sketchbook and binoculars with me…"

He gestured at his bag, but Mr Deacon was already nodding. "Certainly! That's an excellent idea. But don't stray too far from the Centre and make sure you're back by four."

As soon as Mr Deacon was out of earshot, Lewis turned to Rhona. "Are you OK? You've gone a funny colour."

"We're in big trouble, Lewis." Rhona's eyes were stricken. "Ailsa McAllister knows that we've seen the dead unicorn."

"How can she?"

A single tear trickled down Rhona's cheek. "It's all my fault."

"I don't understand. What's going on? Is it because of the medallion?"

"I didn't lose the medallion abseiling, Lewis. And Ailsa didn't find it at the cliff... I gave my St Christopher to the unicorn."

"You did what?"

Rhona tried to explain, tears spilling down her face. "He looked so tragic. I wanted to leave some kind of tribute. You know the way people leave flowers at roadside accidents? I took off my medallion and tucked it into his mane. That horrible girl found it. And now she knows it's mine. She knows I was there."

Lewis gulped, closed his eyes.

Ailsa McAllister has a gun. She doesn't want people to know about the dead unicorn. She knows we know. We should keep well away from her. But...

He breathed in the soft mountain air, tried to gather his rapidly unravelling courage.

"Rhona, I'm going to the Langcroft Estate, right now, before the others come back." He spoke quickly, getting the words out before he had time to change his mind.

"I reckon it's where Ailsa is holding the other unicorns we heard her talk about. I know it's a crazy plan, and you don't need to come with me if you don't want to. But I'm going to find the unicorns, and when I find them, I'm going to set them free."

He hoisted his rucksack on to his shoulders and set off across the moor, trying to ignore the fear gripping his insides.

12

Rhona

Rhona watched Lewis go, too shocked to move.

Had he really just said he was going to go to Langcroft and free the unicorns?

Her Lewis?

What had got into him?

He usually moved at a sluggish pace, head down, hair drooping, but this afternoon he was like a different person, striding across the heather, focused and determined, heading straight for trouble.

"Oi, wait for me!" Rhona chased after him, deciding she'd better be the voice of reason. "Haud on, Lewis. For starters, you don't even know where Langcroft is. Shouldn't we go back to the Centre first an' get a map?"

Lewis didn't slow down. He kept walking, so fast that Rhona had to scurry to keep up. "I know exactly where Langcroft is. We passed the entrance when we were going kayaking. I noticed because I've always wanted to go there. Langcroft House is world-famous for the sculptures in its walled garden. There's even a Henry Moore."

"Oh, wow. A Henry Moore, whatever the heck that is, and fifteen flamin' unicorns. So what's the plan, Lewis? Should we no' have a plan? Or are we just going to march into Langcroft and say 'Oi, big man, let a' those unicorns go?'"

Lewis chewed his bottom lip and Rhona's heart plummeted. Surely that wasn't the actual plan.

"I think we might need a more subtle approach," he said, clearly making the plan up as he went along. "The gates will be open, as the estate gardens are open to the public, but once we're inside, we'll have to do a bit of sneaking around."

"Aye, we'll have to be sneaky alright. Ailsa knows we've seen the deid unicorn. Bet she's expecting us to turn up." Rhona banged her fist against her forehead. "I can't believe I was such a numpty! I could have picked some heather or something. Why did I have to leave evidence that I was at the actual scene of the actual crime?"

Lewis shrugged. "It was a nice gesture. And Ailsa McAllister might know we saw the unicorn's body, but there's nothing she can do about it, is there? I bet she's a lot more scared than we are. She'll be afraid that we're running about telling people."

"We tried that, didn't we? Mr Deacon didn't believe a word we said. And no wonder."

An appalling thought occurred to her, so horrible it made her feel physically sick.

"Lewis, what if Ailsa has hacked off the horns? She wouldn't have to hide the unicorns if she's done that, would she? They'd look like bog-ordinary horses."

"I don't know for sure, but I don't think they'd survive that." Lewis started to walk even faster, as if he was trying to outrun the danger.

Rhona trailed behind in gloomy silence, dreading what they were going to find.

It seemed a long walk and Rhona wasn't sure if Lewis was even heading in the right direction, but large white lettering spelling 'Langcroft Estate' loomed into view. Lewis pointed at it, eyes triumphant.

"We're here!"

"Well spotted, Sherlock."

They walked through the main gate, towards a forest of signs. Lewis stopped in front of them.

"So where first: the car park, the walled garden, the main house, the café, the children's play area or the public toilet?" he asked.

"Don't be daft," said Rhona. "We need to look in the

non-touristy places. Let's try this way." She veered off, onto a narrow path, lined with ragged Scots pines. Lewis followed. It felt good to be taking the lead, though she'd have been happier if she'd a clue where to go.

"Where would be the best place to keep a herd of unicorns?" asked Lewis. "Do you think they'll have split them up or kept them all together?"

Rhona resisted the urge to ask him how she was supposed to know that and focused on negotiating the path ahead. Though she'd never have admitted it to Lewis, it was clear that the shortcut through the trees wasn't the best idea she'd ever had. The rutted tracks were dangerously uneven and they had to walk with their eyes turned down to avoid being tripped by snaking roots or snagged by trailing brambles. It seemed to take forever before the trees cleared and they arrived at the edge of a small loch. In the distance they could see Langcroft house itself, its sandstone turrets gleaming butter-yellow in the sunshine. Rhona was relieved to be back in the sunlight, but they were in more danger here.

They started to walk along the loch, heading further from the house, towards another area of woodland. Rhona pointed out a dilapidated boathouse crouched by the water.

"What about in there?"

The building's corrugated-iron roof was rusted and

pitted with holes, the slatted walls badly split and the paintwork long peeled away.

Rhona gave the door a gentle push. It creaked open. Sunlight washed over the interior, formed puddles of molten silver on the ground, and for a moment it seemed as though magic was a possibility. But closer inspection revealed the upturned hull of a wrecked rowing boat, some broken oars and a heap of rusting tools.

"No unicorns." Rhona bit her lip, bizarrely disappointed. For a split second, the boathouse had seemed the perfect place to keep a couple of unicorns, but now she could see that it was completely unsuitable. The roof was too low, the space too cramped. Unicorns were big animals. They needed space.

"Ah, well." She shrugged. "Nobody said unicorn hunting was easy."

As she closed the shed door, a fragment from Alex's story drifted across her brain.

Look carefully and you'll see them. Stone unicorns are everywhere...

"It's probably a waste of time, but let's try the walled sculpture garden," she suggested. "We'll have to be really careful though."

"Don't get me wrong, Rhona, I'd love to see the sculptures, but how on earth is that going to help us find the unicorns?"

"Don't you remember the end of Alex's story? He said there are statues of unicorns all over Scotland. D'you no' think there'll be one in Langcroft's famous sculpture garden?"

"I guess so, though I'm not sure how finding a statue will get us any closer to finding the real thing."

Rhona shrugged. She wasn't sure either, but she had a feeling that it might give them some sort of clue. "Have you a better idea, pal?"

Lewis grinned at her. "Nope. Let's do it."

But Rhona's heart was thumping against her ribs as they drew nearer to the big house. What if Ailsa was watching them from one of those upstairs windows?

There were a few visitors about, and nobody paid them any attention or asked to see their tickets as they strolled casually through the stone archway into the walled garden. As soon as Rhona entered, she felt a change in the atmosphere. The garden felt safe, enclosed, and the air was heavy with the scent of roses.

It was a serene, beautiful place. Lewis and Rhona walked together, with Lewis occasionally letting out an appreciative gasp or remark when he came across a sculpture.

While Lewis was staring, awe-struck, at some black marble, Rhona came to a hedge that had once been trimmed into an archway, but was now so badly overgrown that she had to push her way through. On the other side, in the corner where the side and back garden walls met, stood a small, neglected statue. Years of exposure to air and moisture had given the bronze a green patina, and its stone plinth was pitted, stained with lichen. At first she thought it was a stallion, rearing on odd cloven hooves, but then she noticed the horn on its forehead, broken almost at the base.

"Lewis!" she called. "Come and see!"

He didn't appear, so she walked slowly around the statue, wondering if this unicorn might hold a clue to the herd's whereabouts. When she ran her hand across its green flanks, she felt for a moment as if it might come to life, but the statue remained motionless, hooves raised, caught in mid-air. Swirling dust motes gleamed like flecks of gold and the air around the statue seemed to shimmer with magic. Heart beating fast, Rhona stepped back and took another look.

Attached to the stone plinth was a badly tarnished plaque. Pulling her jacket sleeve down over her hand, Rhona rubbed hard at it. For a moment, nothing happened. All she'd achieved was another filthy mark on her jacket. But as she stared, centuries of dirt and wear began to vanish, fade away as if she'd wiped the silver with some incredible cleaning fluid, the sort of product they advertise on the shopping channels. The plaque gleamed, its bright surface etched with curvy, scrolled letters.

> Open the back door, enter the wood,
> Take the path where deer once stood.
> Find Dubhar's statue carved from beech
> And what you seek's within your reach.

She had just finished reading when she heard Lewis struggling to get through the hedge behind her. "Hurry up, Lewis! I'm in here! Something weird just happened."

But by the time he'd reached the statue the words had vanished, as if they'd never existed. The plaque had returned to the way it was before, and although she gave it another rub, nothing changed.

Rhona grabbed at Lewis's arm. "You're going to think I'm blethering, but I rubbed the plaque under the statue an' writing appeared. It was a verse, and it said that to find the unicorns we need to follow the path where the deer once stood, until we get to another statue, a wooden one. That plaque said so. I swear it did," she said, desperate to convince him that the impossible had just happened.

Lewis nodded, and she realised she didn't have to try and convince him. After all, he'd seen a real live unicorn.

"OK. Let's go. Um, Rhona, what's happened to the archway?"

She spun round. It was as if the hedge had repaired itself.

The gap had gone, replaced by glossy-leaved, dense foliage.

"This is getting weirder by the minute," she muttered.

Directly behind the statue was the garden's rear wall, and set into the wall was a door, half-hidden by ivy.

The back door! she thought.

"This way," she said, sounding more definite than she felt, and ran over to it.

She rattled the handle. It was locked; of course it was. The McAllisters wouldn't want trespassers in their woods. She tugged at the ivy covering the wall, checking to see if it would take their weight.

"You're not seriously planning on climbing that wall?"

"Well, what's your cunning plan?"

A sharp click made them both jump. They turned in the direction of the sound, half-expecting to see Ailsa standing there, gun cocked. But the click came from the door. It was swinging silently open. For a moment they both stood frozen, stunned.

Rhona broke the silence, her voice a whisper. "This is *so* weird."

"Yes, but it's good weird. Let's go."

13

Lewis

Fear snaked down Lewis's spine. The tiny hairs on the back of his neck rose. He didn't understand what was going on, but he could feel anger in the air, a terrible rage that didn't belong to him, and he didn't think was Rhona's.

"Lewis, do you think this place is magic? Maybe Ailsa's a real live witch."

He shook his head. There was nothing magical about her. Ailsa's greed and cruelty were only too human.

"There's something magical happening here," he said, "but it isn't the place, it's the unicorns. Can't you feel their anger buzzing? It's like the noise you hear when you stand close to a pylon."

"Is that what that is?"

"I think they want us to find them, and to help them escape. I mean, they haven't told me so or anything.

I can sense it, if that makes any sense." He stood up, stared around and then pointed westward. "See those tufts of spiky grass? The ground's really spongy. I think it might follow the path of an old stream. We're looking for a path that deer used to use, aren't we? Could that be where deer used to come to drink?"

Rhona leapt up, animated once more. "Hurry up, Lewis! We haven't got time to sit about, you lazy git! Mr Deacon will have a hairy fit if we're late back."

Through the wood they squelched, following the boggy path.

Then Lewis saw a large, oddly shaped object, half hidden in the undergrowth. It was a crudely carved unicorn, green with moss, blown or knocked over. The unicorn's front hooves were sunk in dead leaves, slowly rotting in the damp ground.

First, Lewis tried to right the unicorn, but it was far too heavy. When that failed, he checked the statue for a plaque, but there was none visible, and no writing was carved on the wood. Rhona searched too, getting increasingly cross.

"How are we meant to find the herd when there aren't any more clues?" she muttered. "We'll need to get back, Lewis. This is a deid end."

He shook his head. How could that be when he could feel hope fluttering in the air, light as butterflies?

"Sit down here, Rhona, please. I think we need to be still for a moment."

For a long moment they sat in silence. When Rhona's body tensed, Lewis realised that she was feeling the magic around them too.

"They know we're comin'," she whispered. Then pointed, suddenly distracted. "Aw look, a squirrel!"

Lightning-quick, the bright-eyed red squirrel scrambled across the statue's back. When it reached the unicorn's horn, it stopped for a second and looked back at them. Its liquid eyes stared straight into Lewis's.

As it scuttled up the trunk of a beech tree, Lewis leapt to his feet.

"That's the clue!" he shouted, his voice echoing round the wood.

Rhona snorted. "Don't be daft. Unicorns can't climb trees."

"No, the unicorn's horn's the clue! It's pointing us in the right direction."

He started running, his feet crunching over dead leaves, hoping Rhona would follow. On and on he ran, dodging between the thin trunks of the birch trees, leaping over stumps, his determination growing with every step.

I can do this. I can keep my promise to the dark unicorn. I'm going to help.

"Lewis! Stop!"

He jumped as though he'd been electrocuted, his bravado dissolving, convinced somebody must be chasing after them, brandishing a gun. But there was nobody there. An ugly red-painted sign was nailed to the tree in front of them:

Danger!
Keep out!

Beech trees in this area are susceptible to sudden branch drop.

14

Rhona

"Let's keep going." Lewis was emphatic. "They're definitely trying to keep people out. They don't want anyone to know what they're up to. Come on."

So they walked on, although Rhona did spot Lewis glancing upwards a few times, whenever a branch creaked.

As they clambered across a tangle of tree roots, a section of barbed-wire fencing that was half hidden in the undergrowth whipped up, flailing across Lewis's jacket sleeve and ripping against his hand. "Ow!"

Rhona grimaced at the sight of the long, bloody scratch.

They kept going, although she was seriously starting to worry that they should be heading back. Lewis might not care, but she wanted to stay in Mr Deacon's good books. How could they stop trying, though, when the air fizzed with hope?

A few minutes later, the trees thinned. Rhona and Lewis entered a clearing. A round wooden structure loomed in front of them, about six metres high and as big as the school's gym hall. It had been built in the centre of the clearing and was made of logs, placed vertically and sharpened at the top. The whole structure was surrounded by a high but oddly insubstantial fence made from thin strands of wire attached at regular intervals to wooden posts.

"Do you think it's a kids' play area?" asked Rhona, though she knew in her heart it was no such thing. Why would anyone build a kids' play area in the middle of nowhere?

"It looks like a stockade, like the Romans made for defence."

Rhona grabbed Lewis's hand, only remembering his injury when he yelped with pain. "Oh, sorry. But Lewis, cowboys built stockades to enclose livestock… This must be where they're keeping the unicorns!"

They listened for the sound of voices, but heard only snorting noises, and the occasional loud bang, as if something was crashing against the log walls.

"They're in there, Lewis," she whispered. She'd never felt so certain of anything in her life. The air surged with expectation. They were in there, and they were waiting for her and Lewis to let them out.

She was about to go further when Lewis grabbed

her jacket. "Stop there, Rhona. That fence is electrified. We'll need to try and crawl underneath it."

She looked again at the fence. It seemed so flimsy. But if it was electrified, getting the unicorns out was going to be impossible. They couldn't crawl underneath and it looked far too high to jump.

Cautiously, desperately afraid in case her puffy jacket should come in contact with the wire, she rolled under it and Lewis followed, slithering snake-like.

"There must be an entrance round the other side," whispered Lewis. "We need to find it."

The logs had been driven into the ground edge to edge, but there were narrow gaps here and there. Rhona peered through one of the slits, her curiosity to see unicorns overcoming her fear.

It was like watching a flickering black-and-white movie. Inside the stockade, everything was monochrome, a moving blend of greys, white and jet-black. She gulped and stepped back a little, overwhelmed by the impression of constant movement, of sharp horns, large beasts turning this way and that, too close for comfort, eyes rolling, lips curling in fear. Up close, the unicorns' pent-up rage and terror was disturbing.

There was nothing cute about the unicorns in that stockade, no rainbow manes, glittery eyelashes or plaited tails. She could sense their hope of release, flickering like light through the bars. All these unicorns wished for was their freedom, to go home to their enchanted forest, and to live in peace.

Lewis's shout made her jump.

"The doors are here! They're barred, and padlocked. I don't think we'll—"

She continued round, following the sound of his voice, until he spoke again, in a very different tone.

"Oh, hi there! You couldn't tell me how to get to the toilets, could you? I've managed to get totally lost!"

Rhona froze, her back pressed against the stockade, wishing she could merge with its wooden walls. Behind her, the unicorns had gone still, as if they were listening too.

Ailsa's voice cut through the silence. "So lost that you crawled under an electric fence?"

"You're kidding! Is the fence electrified? I had no idea. Wow, wasn't it lucky that I didn't electrocute myself?"

"Members of the public are strictly prohibited from entering this area of the estate. You've walked for miles out of your way. Can't you read signs, you stupid brat?"

"I can read perfectly well, thanks, but I'm desperate for a pee and I'd be really grateful if you'd tell me the way to the toilets."

There was another long silence, broken only by one of the unicorns breathing down its long nose close to

Rhona's ear. Even through the bars of the stockade she could feel its power, its wild magic, and it made her shiver.

When Ailsa spoke again, her voice dripped icicles. "I know who you are. You're not fooling anyone. Where's your wee fat friend? Is she sneaking around too? You're both trespassing, and around here, trespassers get shot."

Rhona scowled.

Fat! Cheeky so-and-so. That polite act with Mr Deacon was pure fakery.

A massive bang split the still air.

For a terrible moment Rhona thought Lewis had been killed, but then she saw him rolling under the fence, haring across the grass towards the cover of the trees. She ran for the fence too, scrambling under, her breath coming in panicky bursts. As she raced into the woodland and crashed through the undergrowth, her heart banging against her ribs, she could hear the trapped unicorns bellowing, their hooves clattering against the walls of the stockade.

15

Lewis

Lewis's heart was pounding against his ribs.

Ailsa would have pulled the trigger. I was about to die…

Rhona caught up with him and they hurried together in grim, determined silence, focused on escape. The thickness of the undergrowth made running hard work.

By the time they reached the outskirts of the wood, Lewis's lungs were bursting. When they neared the big house they slowed to a jog, which they kept up until they were out of the main gates of Langcroft and back on the moorland road.

Even then they walked fast, though Rhona's cheeks were crimson blotches, her breathing ragged. They strode until she bent double, clutching her side.

"I've got a gowpin' stitch. I need to stop."

She flung herself down on the damp grass, exhausted.

For a couple of minutes, she lay, breathing hard, and then got back on her feet. "OK, sorted. What happened back there? I thought you were a goner!"

"Ailsa pointed the gun at me. Maybe she was just trying to scare me, but I really thought she was going to shoot. Then one of unicorns went nuts. It made this trumpeting noise, like an elephant, and its hooves crashed against the walls, so hard one of the logs split and came down on Ailsa's arm. She fell and I ran for it. I don't know if she got hurt."

"Wow. You owe your life to a unicorn. That's pretty amazing."

Lewis nodded, and then felt guilt creep over him. "I'm really sorry I ran off and didn't check you were following me. I kind of assumed…"

"You did the right thing. I was hardly going to wait around for Ailsa to start shooting, was I? I don't need you to be flamin' Prince Charming, Lewis. I'm no' Cinder-ruddy-ella." Her eyes were bright with tears. "It's no' right, Lewis. We can't let that girl get away with it. We have to do something. We have to get the unicorns away from her!"

He nodded. Fear squirmed, an eel in his chest. He looked down at the nasty scratch on the back of his hand. He was lucky that the scratch was his only injury. Still, despite his fear, he agreed with Rhona. Ailsa couldn't be allowed to get away with it. They had to try and rescue the unicorns. But how?

"Look, there's the bus!" shouted Rhona, pointing ahead. It was rumbling towards the Outdoor Centre. "They're all back from the gorge walk. We'd better run."

Rhona and Lewis reached the car park as the rest of the group were jumping down from the bus, chattering excitedly about their day out. They mingled with the others, and Mr Deacon barely noticed their arrival because Miss James was telling him all about Derek's disastrous attempt to climb up the side of the gorge. She looked shattered, and Lewis had a feeling this might be the last time she volunteered to go on a residential trip.

"First thing I knew of it was when I heard this massive splash," she said, sounding close to tears. "He was lucky he wasn't swept downstream to his death. How I'd have explained that to his mother, I don't know!"

"I don't suppose 'It served him right' would have been good enough for his doting parent, but it would have been accurate," sighed Mr Deacon.

Derek poured muddy water from his wellies onto the gravel.

Dinner was delicious: lasagne and chips, followed by caramel shortcake and custard. The fantastic food was almost enough to make Lewis reconsider his dislike of residential trips. Hardly anyone spoke during the meal. They all seemed shattered after the gorge walk, and Ellie Morris nearly fell asleep in her bowl of custard. It was so oddly quiet that even a whispered conversation with Rhona was out of the question. Lewis shovelled food into his mouth and tried to come up with a plan, but he seemed to be right out of ideas.

Face facts, he thought miserably. *You can't do this. You made a promise to the unicorn you aren't going to be able to keep.*

For an hour after dinner, the pupils read or played board games in the common room. Lewis, unable to focus on either his book or his worries, watched Derek and Tariq play a noisy game of Jenga. Then Scott wheeled out the karaoke machine and Mr Deacon began murdering 'My Way' and a million other songs from the olden days. Lewis sat beside Rhona on a couch and kept glancing out of the windows, looking for inspiration in the starlit sky. But it wasn't forthcoming.

"I can't listen to any more of this mince," muttered Derek, who was sitting opposite, throwing Maltesers in the air and catching them in his mouth. He leapt up, wrestled the mike from Mr Deacon and sang a surprisingly tuneful rendition of 'Caledonia', but he'd scarcely finished when Mr Deacon grabbed the microphone back.

"I almost forgot to say! I've got terrific news for you all!" he bawled. "I've managed to wangle an invite to the Langcroft Estate tomorrow for some team-building activities! Isn't that fantastic?"

He beamed, clearly very impressed with himself, but the reaction was rather muted. Everyone else seemed too exhausted to relish the prospect of team-building activities in the morning. But Lewis felt a current of excitement shoot up his spine, and when he looked at Rhona she was sitting up straighter, a massive grin spreading across her face.

"I can't believe I'd forgotten," she whispered. "We're going back to Langcroft in the morning. We've got another chance!"

Lewis grinned too. Ideas were whizzing around his brain like racing bikes on a circuit.

We can go back to the stockade… We can break down the doors… We can free the unicorns… But how?

Mr Deacon was still yelling into the microphone.

"Someone really ought to explain to him how microphones work," Lewis groaned, but Rhona shushed him.

"It's quiz time!" she yelled. "Derek, Ellie, get yourselves over here. You can be part of team Ginger Ninjas!"

Lewis sighed and took one of the quiz sheets from Max's hand. How was he supposed to focus on the unicorns *and* do a stupid quiz?

But it turned out to be great fun, in a fiercely competitive sort of way. The article he'd read in the magazine was really useful during the 'all about Scotland' round, and he excelled during the art and literature round. Derek was brilliant at answering music and sport questions, and Ellie seemed to know everything about animals and science. Rhona didn't answer many questions, but she wrote down the answers in her untidy scrawl and whooped enthusiastically every time their team won a point, much to Flora's obvious annoyance. By the end of the final round, their team was neck and neck with Flora's.

"Right, guys," shouted Scott. "Tie-breaker question! A herd of cows... A flock of sheep... What do we call a group of unicorns?"

"That's not fair," whined Flora, throwing down her pencil. "Unicorns aren't real animals!"

Lewis bit his lip, annoyed with himself for having no idea.

Derek nudged Ellie. "You're the animal expert, Ell."

Ellie shrugged helplessly. "Haven't the foggiest."

Rhona was sitting quietly for once, chewing the end of the pencil. Suddenly she scribbled on the quiz sheet, jumped up and threw herself across the room.

Scott held up their paper.

"Correct answer. A blessing of unicorns! The Ginger Ninjas win tonight's quiz. Come and get your prize, guys!"

Flora glowered and muttered about cheating, while Derek punched the air, his face glowing with delight.

"Ya dancer! I've never won anything in my whole life! This is the best week ever!"

As they collected their box of chocolates, Lewis flung his arm round Rhona's shoulder.

"That was amazing! How on earth did you know the answer to that one?" he asked.

Rhona laughed. "I was thinking about unicorns and the word 'blessing' popped into my brain. Weird, but like you said, good weird. We won! Class bit of teamwork, wasn't it?"

"I bagsy the strawberry creams!" yelled Derek, holding the chocolate box up like a trophy. "We are the champions!"

When the time came for lights out, the excitement of winning the quiz was beginning to fizzle, and as Lewis lay in the darkness, a sense of hopelessness settled over him like fog. Teamwork might have helped this evening, but even if he had a crack SAS team at his disposal, he knew he'd still be struggling to come up with a plan to rescue the unicorns.

16

Lewis

In the early morning Lewis was woken by Max, banging on the door.

"Time to get up, lads! Exciting day ahead!"

Exciting didn't exactly cover it. Terrifying… dangerous… life-threatening…

In the harsh light of day it seemed as if he'd taken on too big a challenge. He pulled the duvet over his face.

Then he felt the duvet being tugged upwards, a blast of cold air. His roommate Kyle was standing by the bed, his face screwed up with anger. He shouted, right in Lewis's face, "Get up, will you! We'll lose points to the girls if your bed isn't made."

Kyle whipped Lewis's pillow from under his head. Lewis grabbed it back, so fast the pillowcase fabric ripped.

He tucked it back under his head. "Um, who cares about stupid points?"

"Come on! Be fair. Why do you have to be like this?" Kyle snatched at the duvet and pulled it right off the bed.

Angry now, Lewis tried to retrieve his covers, but Kyle called for reinforcements and his mates Ben and Tariq rushed over. Tariq grabbed the back of Lewis's T-shirt and started to haul him from the bed while he wriggled and struggled. Ben and Kyle took a leg each, dragged him off the bed and plonked him down on the floor.

Kyle looked down at Lewis, his lip curled, trying to look tough. "We care, loser."

"Yes, and that's entirely up to you," said Lewis, sitting up, trying to maintain his dignity. "But I'm not interested in your petty point-scoring. It's totally lame."

The three boys circled him. Kyle looked like he'd happily murder him, but Tariq just looked baffled.

"I don't get it," he said, running a hand through his tousled hair. "Why do you always want to ruin things for everyone? What the heck is wrong with you, Lewis?"

Lewis scrambled to his feet, held up his hands. "Um, overreaction here, guys?"

Kyle threw the pillow at him and it bounced off his head.

"Oi, that's enough."

They all spun round. Mr Deacon was standing in

the doorway. Derek McIvor was behind him, shuffling anxiously from foot to foot. Lewis realised he'd been rescued by Derek the Dweeb.

"Look at the state of this place," said Mr Deacon. "Put that bedding back. Lewis, get dressed."

"That was always the plan," grumbled Lewis. "I was just waiting for this lot to back off."

"Right now, Lewis!"

Despite being chilled to the bone in his T-shirt and boxers, he took his time in getting dressed and wandered down to the breakfast room a good five minutes after everyone else. He didn't want them to think they'd won. Rhona waved at him, gestured towards a chair. He sat down, still seething.

"You'd think group points were life and death, the way they carry on."

Rhona shot him a look. "Have you been annoying the other lads again?" she sighed. "Why don't you just play along, Lewis?"

"I prefer to do my own thing. What's so wrong with that, eh?"

Rhona clicked her tongue. "It doesn't hurt to think of other people sometimes."

"Good news, kids!" Scott stood up, smiling his toothpaste-advert smile. "I've had a phone call from Alex McAllister at Langcroft, firming up our invitation. We're going to take part in a raft-building challenge! Finish up your brekkie and go get on your gear!"

Lewis sighed. "It'll be OK. Or at least, the stupid raft-building challenge will be hellish, but among the others we'll be safe enough from Ailsa."

As the minibus rumbled along the single-track road, he stared out of the window, still trying to come up with a plan. How could he get the unicorns out of the stockade and over an electric fence? It wasn't possible.

He shuddered, reliving those terrifying seconds when he'd stood at the stockade, helpless, while Ailsa pointed a gun at him. Despite what he'd said to Rhona, there was a real risk they'd see Ailsa McAllister at Langcroft. And despite Rhona's attempts to hide herself yesterday, the chances were that Ailsa would recognise her. The white jacket and the ginger hair were fairly standout. And Ailsa would definitely recognise him, having met him twice already. They'd need to be very careful.

The minibus turned off the main road, through the pillared gateposts. It reached the huge sandstone mansion house, trundled downhill towards the ornamental lake and shuddered to a halt. They all piled out.

A tall, gangly young man strolled over and stood in front of the group. Lewis had never seen him before in his life, but he recognised the voice immediately.

"Hi, guys. I think most of you met me the other night,

but for any who don't know, I'm Alex McAllister. I've been asked to organise this morning's activities. The plan is to get into four teams. First team to build a raft and successfully launch it gets the prize! Who's in?"

Lewis nudged Rhona. "You were right. It's him," he whispered. "It's the guy from the Land Rover. Ailsa's brother."

Rhona nodded, but didn't take her eyes off Alex. He kept talking, oblivious to them. "After the raft building, we'll warm up with hot chocolate and a picnic on the beach." This information was greeted with a loud chorus of cheers. "My uncle, the Laird, might pop over to say hello at some point, so remember your manners, guys. Right, I'm going to hand over to your instructors, so they can organise the teams."

Lewis didn't even flinch when he found out he was in the same team as Flora. It just seemed inevitable. And the raft building was a disaster, as he'd known it would be.

The task was meant to be about teamwork and co-operation, but ended in a massive fight when their team's totally rubbish raft upended and tipped Flora into the loch. She splashed out of the water, dragging a sodden rope behind her, face contorted with rage, hair in wet, snaky tendrils, like Medusa's. Her gorgon eyes flashed with fury.

"His knots were rubbish! They all came undone!"

Rhona stormed over, leaping to Lewis's defence as usual. "It was a team challenge, you bampot. It wasn't Lewis's fault you capsized the raft. Your paddling was pure mince."

Flora achieved a mean impersonation of Lewis's voice, vowels clipped, posh as the Queen's: "*I can tie knots*, he said. *I learned in Anchor Boys.* Loser." She even flicked her hair the way Lewis did when he was nervous. But she didn't go any further. When they were in Primary 5, she'd gone too far and Lewis told her he'd report her to the Head for racist bullying. She'd bawled at him that he couldn't take a joke, but the Head hadn't found Flora's 'jokes' remotely funny either.

Rhona had her own strategy for dealing with bullies. She raised her fists. "Shut your trap, Flora, or I'll dunk you back in head first."

Flora wisely shut it.

"Don't listen to her." Rhona took Lewis's arm in hers. "She's just ragin' cos we beat her in the quiz." She stuck her tongue out at Flora and marched Lewis out of range.

"Rhona, I'm not bothered, honestly. We've got more important things to worry about than Flora."

Behind them, an engine revved, car tyres rumbled. Rhona looked up and her grip on Lewis's arm tightened. "Aw, no… look."

A battered khaki Land Rover was careering away from

the big house, rattling over a cattle grid and hurtling up the road that ran towards the main gate.

"It's Ailsa," whispered Rhona. "She's leaving! We've got to do it now, Lewis, while she's away. This is our chance to rescue the unicorns."

Lewis didn't speak. He stared after the vehicle. One of its doors had a massive dent in it, more a hole than a dent, as if it had been slammed by a battering ram. Or speared by a unicorn's horn.

17

Rhona

It was hard to enjoy a ham and pickle piece when she was sick with nerves. Rhona was chilled to the bone after the raft building, so the hot drink was welcome, although she spilled some over her already manky jeans when Alex McAllister leapt to his feet right in front of her.

"Oh, hello, Uncle!" he called. "I wondered if you'd join us this morning!"

The Laird was rosy-cheeked, white-haired and bearded, and wore a waxed jacket, kilt and Timberlands. Accompanying him were two lolloping black Labradors. He patted his nephew on the back and waved cheerily at the group on the beach.

"He's like a garden gnome," said Flora through a mouthful of sandwich. Miss James glared, but Flora was right enough. He just needed a red hat and a fishing rod.

The Laird beamed at them, waving his walking stick in the air. "Welcome to Langcroft, boys and girls! I hope you're having a wonderful time here!"

"It's very decent of you to allow us to use your grounds," said Mr Deacon.

"It's absolutely no trouble, I assure you! Please feel free to walk around…"

"He seems harmless," whispered Rhona.

Lewis looked thoughtful and glugged his hot chocolate. "He's allowed this to happen though, hasn't he? Even if his intentions were good, by agreeing to Ailsa stealing the unicorns he's put them in danger. He should have left them alone. He should have left them in Whindfall Forest, where they belong."

Rhona nodded.

"Right, guys." Scott stood up. "The Laird has kindly invited us on a walk to see the Salmon Leap. Gather up your stuff. Let's go!"

As the others started filing after the teachers and the Laird, Lewis tugged at Rhona's sleeve.

"We can't go with them. We've got one chance to save the unicorns, Rhona."

She nodded, her heart thumping in her chest. Mr Deacon was going to be so mad at them, but still…

So they lagged behind, and when the others headed towards the riverbank, they hid behind a tree and waited until the rest of the group were out of sight.

"I've got an idea. There's no use goin' empty-handed," said Rhona. "Come on!"

"Rhona, we've already looked in there," Lewis grumbled as she opened the door of the boathouse.

She raked through the heap of tools she'd spotted last time until she found what she needed.

"An axe? Who are you planning to behead?"

"Gie me a hand, Lewis. It weighs a ton."

With Lewis's help, Rhona lugged the heavy implement. Being armed, even with a rusty axe, gave her more confidence, but negotiating the woods was still a difficult challenge. Twice Rhona had to drop the axe in the undergrowth in case she terrified a passing tourist.

Eventually they reached a fence marked:

Once they'd clambered over it, the paths disappeared. The electric current of expectation that Rhona had felt in the air yesterday was gone. She sensed that the unicorns had lost hope.

At one point she attempted to psych herself up by waving the axe like a warrior Pict, but it was too heavy, flipped backwards and scraped against the ground. It seemed like a bad omen, as if the task they'd set themselves was too big.

"Do you want to go back?" she asked Lewis, but the look he gave her was adamant. She nodded and walked on.

She imagined the uncomplicated laugh she could have had on the walk with the rest of the group to the Salmon Leap. This week was supposed to be her respite, her escape from worry and responsibility, but now she was being pulled in a very different direction. Who was doing the pulling? Was it the unicorns, or her own heart?

Her shoulders sagged with relief when they came across the unicorn carving and knew they were going in the right direction. As she walked past it, she felt the atmosphere change. There was that hum of expectation.

Lewis must have felt it too. "They know we're coming," he said.

As the pair walked on, the clouds drifted apart and the sun peeped through, making wet leaves shimmer and the grass glisten, jewel-bright. Somewhere in the trees, a woodpecker drummed.

"It feels magical in here, like an enchanted forest," she whispered.

Lewis laughed. "Or it might just be a bog-standard wood with added unicorns."

When they finally reached the stockade, Rhona took a deep breath, caught between anticipation and fear.

Every muscle tensed, she crept forward and shimmied under the fence, dragging the axe behind her. Lewis followed. Once beside the stockade, Rhona let the axe drop, glad to be free of its weight.

"Let's see if we can switch off the electric fence first," she said.

Lewis nodded, and together they walked around the perimeter of the stockade until Lewis stopped at a metal box on a pole beside the fence.

"That's the security box. The energiser will be in there."

Rhona reached towards it.

"Don't touch!"

Lewis tugged the hood of her jacket so hard she fell backwards.

She scrambled to her feet, furious. "What was a' that about?"

Lewis shrugged. He didn't appear remotely sorry about sending her flying. "It's live, Rhona."

"What do you mean?"

"See that lightning symbol? It means you'll get an electric shock if you touch the box. I guess it's to stop people from vandalising it or stealing the energiser inside.

It'll have an insulated key, but I expect Ailsa keeps that."

"You mean we can't switch off the fence?"

"No. We could try and short-circuit it, but I'm not sure how. I'd need to google instructions and I haven't got my mobile."

They both stood, statue-still, staring at one another, trying to think of a solution, when there was none. Then she remembered the axe. She ran over to it and picked it up in both hands.

"Are you planning to chop down one of the posts?" Lewis asked. "You could create a gap that way, but I'm not sure it would be wide enough for the unicorns to escape through."

"That would take all day long, you eejit."

Inside the stockade, the unicorns had become restless. The air swirled with their feelings: rage, frustration, longing, hope.

Rhona didn't speak aloud; instead she let her thoughts fly across the barricade, and hoped that the unicorns would somehow sense her intentions: *I'm going to smash the lock.*

It was as if the whole world was waiting. Birdsong ceased, the breeze dropped and, within the stockade, a deep silence fell.

Rhona stood in front of the doors, wiped both palms on her jeans and swung the axe.

The first blow missed the padlock completely, splintering against wood.

Lewis stopped studying the fence, ran forward and took hold of the shaft of the axe.

"Good plan. Let's do it together. We'll get a better lift. Ready? Aim for the shackle."

"Naw... really?"

The noise of the axe clanging against metal, bashing into wood, was horrendous. Between each attempt, Rhona raised her head and listened, waiting for Alex, Ailsa or the Laird to rush up and demand to know what they were doing.

The iron shackle was crushed and crumpled, but the lock still held, and they were running out of time. Together, they raised the axe again, brought it down as hard as they could. The axe head cracked against iron, then spun off its shaft, sailed through the air and thudded into the side of an old beech tree.

For a long, terrible moment, they stood in silence, unable to process this disaster. Then Rhona let go off the axe handle, and clamped her hands over her mouth, stifling a sob.

"It's over." Lewis let the axe shaft fall. "The axe is wrecked."

"We must have weakened the lock, surely?" Rhona was desperate to hold on to hope.

"Maybe, but it's held." Lewis's voice was brisk, but she could tell his heart was breaking.

And then, from inside the stockade, there was a series of crashes so loud Rhona gasped.

"They're trying to break out!" yelled Lewis, running back towards the front of the stockade.

As Rhona raced to the doors, she saw he was right.

There was no need for her and Lewis to finish the job of breaking the lock. The unicorns were doing that for themselves. Again and again, a mass of hooves crashed against the double doors. The wood bent, the crumpled hasp broke apart and the padlock clattered to the ground. There was a splintering of wood and one of the doors fell with a massive bang, sending clouds of dust into the air.

Rhona leapt back towards the wall, dragging Lewis with her, as the unicorns surged out of the stockade and galloped around it. It was like a stampede, but the animals weren't panicking, or leaderless. A tall female, the lead mare, led the charge. By their fifth circuit, they'd built up speed and that's when the mare jumped, soaring like Pegasus over the electric fence. She whinnied at the others to follow and one by one they did, leaping, as smooth and confident as racehorses, then galloping away through the silver birch trees, immediately camouflaged, almost invisible. Both children stood stock-still, frozen in wonder. Rhona's hands were clenched tight, her body taut as a wire, terrified that one of the unicorns might misjudge the leap and hit the electrified fence. As each one jumped, the smile on her face grew wider.

"Keep going! Keep going!" she whispered, counting them out. "Twelve, thirteen…"

The unicorns were focussed on escape, but the last to jump, a young ash-grey colt with a silver mane and a horn like polished pewter, reared, rolled his eyes and snorted, and then trotted towards them. Majestic and powerful, he stood in front of them, one cloven hoof pawing at the ground, his dark eyes gazing into theirs, radiating magic.

Liath…

The word swirled in the dust and leaves, then drifted away, carried by the breeze.

Liath bowed his head, and then leapt over the fence and galloped after the herd, leaving Rhona and Lewis standing alone in the stockade. They watched, silent, open-mouthed in awe, until the last unicorn was a distant blur.

"Oh, wow. He was saying thank you, Lewis."

"I think you're right." He turned to Rhona. "Well, pal! We did it! We saved the unicorns!"

"I told you teamwork isn't so terrible. You should try it more often."

He didn't sneer at her, just nodded his head and gave

her a sheepish smile. "Bet they're heading for Whindfall Forest!"

"Let's hope they get there before Ailsa realises they've gone."

"And we'd better get back."

But Rhona shook her head and walked into the stockade. The air was foetid, the ground splattered with dung, and it was empty. There were no unicorns left in there.

Lewis called, his voice tinged with worry. "Rhona, we need to go! What are you doing?"

She stomped out of the stockade and faced him, hands on her hips.

"Weren't you counting? Ailsa said she'd nicked sixteen unicorns, an' one of them was pregnant. The stallion's deid, so that leaves fifteen. I've just counted fourteen unicorns in there, and none of them was expectin'. One of the mares is missing. We need to find her."

18

Lewis

Lewis shook his head in disbelief. Rhona could not be serious. They'd just risked their lives to save the unicorns. For a moment, he'd felt massively proud that together they'd achieved something incredible – and, he had to admit, he'd felt relieved that it was over. But now, according to Rhona, it wasn't over after all.

"You can't be sure, in all that chaos. Maybe you miscounted." He could hear a self-pitying whine in his voice, and felt ashamed of it. "And even if you're right and there's another unicorn, we can't look for her now. Mr Deacon is going to be fuming about us sneaking off."

They began to walk, Lewis's head dizzy with the memory of the unicorns streaming out of the stockade, galloping through the woods towards freedom.

He and Rhona were almost at the loch when they heard

a booming voice. "Rhona! Lewis! Where on earth have you been? Will you get down here now!"

Mr Deacon sounded as though he was bellowing into a megaphone. They could hardly pretend they hadn't heard him. Slowly, reluctantly, they headed along the water's edge. Rhona trailed along behind Lewis, kicking sand and pebbles so they sprayed in the air and hit against his calves.

He spun round, ready to yell at her to give over. But then he saw her face. Her hood was up, her chin down. Lewis recognised that defeated look, because he'd seen it before.

When they were both in Primary 3, at three o'clock in the afternoon the Infants' door would burst open like a party popper and they'd all stream out. Rhona would thunder towards the gate, whirling a skipping rope like a lasso, then gaze round, eyes bright and hopeful, at the parents clustered under their umbrellas. Her expression would darken, her mouth would set in a line, and she'd turn and stomp back across the playground towards the waiting teachers. Lewis never got to go home at 3 p.m. either, but he knew Mum was at work and she'd pick him up from after-school care later.

"Mummy not here?" Miss McKay would sigh as Rhona slunk over, dragging her school bag. "I expect she got caught up in the traffic."

The teacher's voice had been bright and brittle. It had been obvious, even to them, a pair of seven year olds, that traffic problems were unlikely to be preventing

127

Rhona's mum making the three-minute walk from her front door to the school gate.

"Maybe she's been run over," Lewis had said. He blushed as he remembered what a little ray of sunshine he'd been, always considering worst-case scenarios first.

"Lewis, there's Mrs Farrell waiting to take you to after-school. Off you go!"

Miss McKay would try and dispatch him before he could invent some other horrible end for Rhona's mother. Rhona would just keep on kicking the penguin-shaped bin in the playground.

"And is it Mum who's supposed to be collecting you? Or your neighbour again, maybe?"

Rhona had never seemed to have a clue who was collecting her, or when.

It must be easier for her now, Lewis thought, *or at least less embarrassing.* After school these days Rhona walked home and let herself in with the key she kept in her school bag.

He couldn't bear to see that old look on her face right now. He put his hand on her shoulder and made her a promise.

"Rhona, we'll find the unicorn. Not now, not this second, but I swear to you, we'll find her and we'll save her. OK?"

The hood lifted. She gave him a watery smile and then her head bobbed back down. He got the feeling she didn't believe a word.

Mr Deacon was apoplectic with rage, but somehow Rhona managed to calm him down with a grim tale about a sudden upset stomach. According to her massive lie, she'd needed to go to the loo urgently and had no time to ask permission… Lewis had apparently been so worried that he'd kindly come with her and waited outside for ages until she'd recovered. She gave so much gruesome detail about her symptoms that Mr Deacon ended up shaking his head vigorously and begging her to stop.

"FTMI, Rhona: far too much information. Are you all right now?"

"I'm brand new, thanks for asking. Did you have a lovely walk, Mr Deacon?"

"Fabulous. The Laird has been telling us all about his conservation projects, haven't you, sir?"

The Laird nodded and gave them all his rosy-cheeked smile.

"And now we have time for a *short* visit to the gift shop," continued Mr Deacon.

Lewis could see desperation in Rhona's eyes. "I'm sure we'll cope without a Langcroft pencil or mug or shortbread tin," he said slowly. "Nobody will be any the wiser if we have a look around."

A smile flickered on Rhona's face. "What about over there?" She pointed towards the old stable blocks opposite the toilets and gift shop. But when they looked more closely, the stalls were cluttered with junk. There was no way a unicorn was hiding among the ancient paint cans and rusting bikes.

As they walked back to the bus, Rhona's steps slowed to a crawl. "Did you hear that? I'm sure I heard a neighing sound."

Lewis strained his ears but could hear nothing. "Leave it, Rhona. Come on."

On the way back in the bus, Lewis stared out of the window, memorising landmarks, noting left turns and right. It would be trickier in the dark. It was only when the bus slowed down at the entrance to the Outdoor Centre that he turned towards Rhona, who was hunched in her seat, sunk in misery.

"We'll go back tonight. Will you be able to get out your room? If not, I can go on my own."

Rhona's head shot up. This time her smile was bright as the sunrise. "No way are you doing this without me!"

The bus shuddered to a halt and Mr Deacon stood up. "Right, everybody out! Check you've left nothing on the seats. Kyle, stop pushing. Archery next! You lucky lot!"

They unbuckled their seatbelts, joining the scramble to leave the bus.

Rhona stopped on the gravel drive. "Are you sure about this, Lewis? You're not scared?"

"Me? Scared of people with guns? What do you think?"

"I think you'd be daft not to be scared, and I shouldn't even have asked such a dumb question."

"Right in one."

"What time will we go?"

"I reckon midnight would be best. Everyone should be asleep by then. It won't take us too long to walk there. We'll look around then get back well before light."

"That sounds OK to me. Maybe half twelve, just to be sure. I'll bring my torch, but the batteries are a bit dodgy."

"I'll bring mine instead. We're sticking together, whatever happens, so we won't need two."

Rhona laughed, and pushed him towards the door.

"Aye, I'll stick with you till the shooting starts. Then you're on your own, pal. My torch is comin' wi' me."

That evening, as soon as dinner was over, everyone rushed off to get ready for the disco. Lewis's mum had packed his black jeans and a white shirt, and he'd told her that she was wasting her time, because there was no way he was going to any lame disco, but Tariq's comment had rattled him.

Why do you always want to ruin things for everyone?

He didn't want to be the sort of person who spoiled everything.

When he was ready, he checked himself out in the long mirror screwed to the dormitory door. Behind him, Derek was carrying on, doing a terrible impersonation of Miss James, while wearing a pair of pants on his head.

"Now, boys and girls! Let me see some super sitting! Oh, my goodness, boys and girls, look at Derek! What a star! Let's make him Pupil of the Week!"

Lewis's reflection grinned, and he blinked in surprise. A couple of days of being outdoors had given his skin a healthy glow, and the smile transformed his face. Under his wire glasses, his eyes sparkled. His newly washed hair was glossy. In his fitted white shirt, he looked, he thought smugly, not too bad at all. He felt like a different person, the new, improved Lewis James Zheng Robertson: quite possibly the only boy in the world who'd seen a unicorn.

By the time Lewis strolled into the common room, the party had started. The room had been decked out with bunting and flashing lights. Some of the girls were dancing, and most of the boys were slouched against the walls, drinking Coke and spluttering with laughter at jokes they weren't sharing with him. He felt his confidence begin to seep away. Maybe *he* was the joke. Maybe they were laughing at *him*.

As he stood there, adjusting his glasses, it dawned on him he'd been wrong. Nothing had changed. He was still the same person, the guy who hated parties, loud noise, lots of people. He was still the outsider, the freak. His head started to throb and he began to back out the door he'd just come in.

"Hi, pal. I got you a Coke!" shouted Rhona, heading over to him carrying two cans, her cloud of frizzy red hair bouncing as she walked. She was wearing a green dress made of silky, floaty material, totally impractical for trekking across a moor.

"Thanks. Nice dress. Is it new?"

Rhona raised her eyes to the ceiling. "Good one, Lewis. Zero out of ten for observation. I picked this dress up in the Dalmarnock Road Oxfam shop for the school Christmas party, *and* wore it to the Easter show."

"Well, it's still nice. Can we get out of here? The noise and the lights are giving me a migraine."

"Did you take one of your painkillers? Take it now, before the migraine takes hold. I'll come outside with you for a bit, but I'm coming straight back. Kayleigh and me have dared each other to get Mr Deacon up to dance!"

She followed him into the deserted corridor, but he could sense her reluctance and felt mean that he'd even asked. His headache wasn't her problem.

Rhona put both her hands on his shoulders. "Lewis, stop stressing. There's no point trying to work out what to do until we know what's happened to the you-know-what. Then we can figure out a plan, based on that info."

She grinned and he nodded.

"Looking fine, Lewis!" Derek barged past them. "We need you on our team for the balloon game! Hurry up, man!"

Reluctantly, Lewis followed Rhona and Derek into the common room.

He wouldn't go as far as to say he had a good time. But the migraine didn't actually materialise, and he laughed a lot, particularly at Mr Deacon's expense, who, it turned out, danced like a malfunctioning robot. And it didn't go on too late. By half past nine they were back in the dorm, getting ready for bed. He and Derek even managed to squeeze in a quick chat about books. He'd had no idea Derek was a Terry Pratchett fan too.

"Have you read *Johnny and the Bomb*? Old, but dead good. You can borrow mine, if you like."

"Aw, thanks, Lewis. You're a real pal."

Lewis squirmed.

I'm no such thing. I've called you horrible names. I've laughed at you.

"I've got *Only You Can Save Mankind* as well. It's brilliant. I'll lend you that one too. Goodnight, Derek."

"Night, Lewis."

Derek pulled his duvet over his lumpy frame and fell asleep almost right away, as did the other boys soon after, despite Derek's gruesome snores.

Lewis lay awake, waiting, his heart thudding like hooves.

19

Lewis

Lewis shook himself out of a doze. His brain felt fuzzy, thick with tiredness. Without his phone he hadn't been able to set an alarm, so he'd tried to stay awake, keeping an eye on his watch, listening to Kyle's grunts and Derek's snores, while trying to create a Top 10 Best Books With a Twist and his Favourite Five Weirdest Animals: anything to stop himself thinking about all the things which could go wrong tonight.

According to his watch's luminous green dial, it was half past twelve. It was time to go. He pulled on a hoodie over his T-shirt, then forced himself to leave the duvet's warmth and scrabble in the dark for his jeans and boots, strewn under the bed.

Surely, he thought as he laced up his boots, *going on a unicorn hunt in the dark has to rank among the craziest things ever done by anyone in the history of the world.*

He was quite proud to feel he was making history.

As he clumped towards the door of the dormitory, it dawned on him that he should have carried his boots and put them on outside. He turned the door handle, trying to avoid making it click.

Behind him, the dormitory seemed to have gone very quiet. Spooked, Lewis turned, door half open, and realised that Derek's snoring had stopped. He was moving. A dark shape bobbed up from under the duvet, like some strange sea creature emerging from the depths.

"You OK?" Derek sounded groggy, three-quarters asleep, but Lewis felt oddly touched by his concern.

"Yeah, I'm fine."

"Where ya goin'?"

"Toilet."

"Right."

Derek pulled the duvet back over his head. Lewis stood for a moment, frozen to the spot, afraid to move. Then, to his relief, the noisy snores restarted, so he tiptoed out, as quietly as his heavy boots would allow, and crept down the corridor towards the common room.

Rhona was already there, huddled in a plastic chair, furry hood up, looking like a ginger Inuit.

"What kept you? I thought I was going to have to enter

the boggin' boys' dorm," she said, her wide grin lighting up her face. "Next problem: how do we get out of here and back in without setting off the alarm?"

"I've figured that out, but you're not going to like it. Forget the bogging boys' dorm, you're going to have to enter the Toilet of Doom. There's a window in there, and it's always open."

"This window has been left open for a very good reason," grumbled Rhona as they entered the boys' toilet. "It smells mingin' in here. Is that the window you meant? How do you expect me to get through that?"

It wasn't easy. Lewis wriggled out first and then jiggled with impatience as he waited for Rhona to squeeze through the tiny, narrow window. What if somebody came in to use the toilet and found Rhona wedged in the window frame? They'd struggle to come up with a good excuse for that one.

"See, you made it," he whispered, shining his torch in her face as she picked herself up off the ground.

"Switch that off, ya bampot, before somebody sees it. Save your battery like I am!" She patted her pocket. "I hope the rest of your plan's more carefully thought out," she grumbled, brushing flecks of paint from her jacket.

"What plan?"

"Very funny. Let's get going. It's freezing out here. Wish I'd brought my gloves."

They walked on the grass so their boots didn't crunch on the gravel. As they left the safety of the Outdoor Centre, Lewis felt a twinge of fear. It was happening. They were putting their lives in danger for an animal that they weren't certain even existed: the fifteenth unicorn.

A full moon hung in the night sky. Stars glittered like frost. It was light enough to see the road's dark surface, the rough grass verges and, in the distance, the looming mountains, fringed with silver moonlight. They weren't going to get lost. Lewis stuffed his torch back in his pocket.

Without the torch to hold, though, his hands fidgeted, zipping and unzipping his jacket, picking at his fingernails. Every snapped twig, every scurrying mouse, made him jump.

"We could sing, if you like," Rhona suggested. "Nobody would hear us out here, 'cept maybe the owls and the badgers and whatever other animals come out at night."

"No, let's not. We wouldn't want to scare the badgers. And the word you were searching for is 'nocturnal.'"

Rhona blew a raspberry and sang tunelessly, just to spite him, then tucked her arm through his.

"We can do this, you know. We're a team." She did a weird war dance, waving her arms and legs in all directions. "I'll be Ninja Girl, the midnight warrior.

You can be my loyal sidekick."

"Um, no, I'm sick of being the sidekick. I'll be Wolf Boy, rescuer of unicorns in distress."

They walked along in the middle of the road, keeping step, their breath forming smoky clouds. Rhona chatted away, telling him all the news from the girls' dorm.

"Flora's no' speakin' to Nasreen... Ellie greets every night because she misses her cat..."

Lewis hardly listened.

What if we run into Ailsa? Or what if the Laird is watching through his windows? What if...

"...Kayleigh and me think Mr Deacon fancies Miss James, but she doesn't fancy him back... Well, who would? He's worn that mingin' cord jacket for all the years I've been at school."

She laughed, the sound loud in the dark.

"Do you remember your first day at Eastgate? Remember how you marched into the playground in that wee green cap and blazer?" She slowed her pace, turned towards him. "Why did you come to Eastgate, Lewis? Were you expelled from your posh school or something? Did you set fire to the bins or smash a window? Were you a mini ned?"

"No, don't be daft." He stopped, unsure if he wanted to share stuff he'd kept to himself for so long. And why was she asking now, when she'd never asked before?

But somehow, it seemed safer to share secrets in the dark.

"Mum and I had to leave our house. My dad… He was basically a good guy, but he had… issues. And one night he lost it."

"What do you mean?"

Lewis sighed, and tried to explain. "He'd been drinking too much for weeks. Mum was getting more and more upset and angry. They were bickering non-stop. And then he just exploded. He was ranting and raving like a crazy person, punching the walls, throwing furniture around. It was horrific…" His voice tailed away.

That time had been horrible, the worst of his life. After The Night Dad Lost It, Mum had whisked Lewis away. He'd had to leave his comfortable home, a big detached house in one of Glasgow's leafy suburbs. He'd had no say at all.

He took a big, gulping breath and carried on.

The Night Dad Lost It, Lewis had cowered under his bed, clutching Carrot, his much-loved stuffed rabbit, while Mum chucked random stuff into binbags and Dad's crazed shouts ricocheted off the walls. When Mum had scooped Lewis up and fled outside to her car, he had dropped Carrot somewhere between his bedroom and the driveway.

"Oh, Lewis. You must have been terrified," said Rhona.

He tried to make a joke, lighten the atmosphere.

"Dropping Carrot is the thing I remember being most gutted about. Though losing him was probably for the best – imagine the kicking I'd have got if I'd brought a soft toy to Eastgate Primary."

"They're not as tough as they make out, Lewis." Rhona strode on, hands stuffed in her pockets, hood up against the chill night wind. "Kyle brought Green Ted to school for years and nobody blinked. He's probably got him in his rucksack at the Centre. So what happened after you left home?"

Lewis stopped walking and gazed up at the star-crusted sky. "I didn't have time to say goodbye to my friends at Bellwood Academy. That night we went to my aunt Lili's. She lives near Edinburgh, miles away."

"Least you were safe there."

Lewis nodded, his stomach churning as the memories came back. He tugged up his hood and quickened his pace, the words flooding out.

For a month they'd stayed at Aunt Lili's, but that was no fun for anyone. Mum had talked about going back to Beijing, her home before she'd come to university in Glasgow and met Dad. Lewis had been quite excited at the prospect of meeting his grandpa, or Wai Gong as Mum called him. But then Mum's friend Maggie had offered her a job and that plan was wiped off the board.

Soon they'd moved again, into a cramped two-bedroom

flat in the East End of Glasgow. That was when he'd lost Bert too, their elderly Border Terrier. Lewis had come home from school one day and Bert was gone: living the perfect dog life, his mother said, and he so hoped it was true, with a retired couple who had a house near the beach.

Lewis had been enrolled at Eastgate Primary, a few streets away from the new flat. He had vivid memories of that first day, walking into the playground in his freakishly neat Bellwood uniform to a chorus of sniggers. It had been so hard, and it hadn't got much easier. Rhona was the only one who seemed to understand.

The truth dawned on him, clear as a Highland sunrise.

"Maybe that's why we get on so well, because my dad and your mum... have the same kind of problems."

Rhona stopped dead in the middle of the road.

"What d'ya mean?" Her face was tight, voice hard with anger. "Are you saying my mum's an alkie? Take that back, or I'll..."

Then she spun, grabbed Lewis's arm and dragged him towards the verge.

"Quick, get down! A car's comin'!"

Lewis's heart banged against his ribs and his brain was spinning. For a terrible moment he'd thought Rhona was attacking him, but she'd been trying to keep him out of harm's way. They huddled behind a stretch of drystone dyke as a battered truck rumbled past, its headlights fuzzy with muck.

When the truck had gone, they stood up and carried on in total silence. Lewis couldn't think what to say to make things better.

Maybe she's in some kind of denial. Her mum has problems, either with drink or drugs. She's never been there for Rhona, ever, all the time I've known her.

One thing was sure: Rhona was absolutely raging with him. How were they were going to find the missing unicorn together when they weren't even speaking?

20

Rhona

He's got no flamin' business badmouthing Mum. Who does he think he is, judging us?

Angry thoughts stomped about in Rhona's brain, kicking the furniture.

There was a tense silence. Rhona only realised she'd wandered off the road when her foot sank into mud. She swore, and Lewis got out his torch and shone it ahead. The sign for the Langcroft Estate glowed in the distance.

As they came nearer, Rhona gasped, ran forward and rattled the gates, which were firmly shut and fastened with a heavy, padlocked chain. When she looked up, she saw that they were topped with long rows of wrought-iron spikes.

She opened her mouth to talk to Lewis, and then remembered she wasn't speaking to him, so walked over to the high wall that encircled the main grounds. The stonework was crumbling in places. If they walked far enough they might find a way in. But time was so short. In a few hours they'd have to get back, or Mr Deacon would be calling the police, the mountain rescue services, the head teacher and their mums. It didn't bear thinking about how much trouble they'd both be in if they didn't return before dawn, or if somebody woke in the night and found their empty beds.

She snatched the torch out of Lewis's hand – "Hey! Use your own!" he whispered – and headed left to a huge oak tree by the wall.

That should be easy to climb, she thought. *We can shoogle along that big overhanging branch and drop down into the garden. It's doable.*

She shoved Lewis's torch in her pocket, swung herself into the tree and started pulling herself up, using the lower branches as footholds. It was only then she remembered that Lewis was terrified of heights. She balanced on a large bough, pointed the torch in his direction and saw him brush his wet fringe out of his eyes, pull back his shoulders. In the torchlight, she could see the fear in his eyes.

He'll just need to get on with it, she thought irritably as she braced herself for the long drop down onto the grass. *He has to, for the unicorn's sake.*

She landed, shone the torch upwards and watched Lewis edge cautiously along the bough of the tree. She could see his reluctance, the tension in his body, and she bounced from foot to foot, caught between impatience and worry.

"Come on, Lewis. We need to go. Hurry!" she hissed.

"I can't," he muttered. "The ground keeps moving. It's getting further away"

In the light of the torch, she noticed his grip on the branch tighten as panic set in.

"You can, Lewis."

She saw him gulp down the fear and start to shuffle further along the bough. She was impressed by his courage. He kept moving forward so that the branch dipped lower and lower, pushed down by his weight, until the leaves on the outer twigs almost brushed the ground.

"Go for it," she hissed. "One, two, three... go."

He leapt and the branch twanged back, smacking against his leg as he tumbled onto the grass, rolled like an acrobat and splatted into a flowerbed. His glasses flew off his face. She couldn't help it. The release of tension was so great that she snorted with laughter as she shone the torch in his eyes.

"Aw, man. You should join a circus."

Lewis picked himself up with as much dignity as he could muster. He retrieved his glasses, dusted mud and dead leaves from his jeans, then gave her a low bow. "I'll learn the trapeze once I've mastered basic clown skills."

"Nice one, pal." She handed him his torch. "Can we go unicorn hunting now?"

"I'm just going to tie my laces, in case I do another pratfall. You go ahead. I'll catch up."

She nodded and strode off into the pine woods, her anger forgotten. Her own dodgy torch stayed in her pocket as she tramped along the moonlit paths. She kept glancing behind to check on Lewis's progress, and she nearly tripped over a passing hedgehog, who panicked and rolled himself into a spiky ball.

"I can still see you. You've just changed shape, not made yourself invisible, you wee numpty."

As she skirted the high walls that enclosed the private gardens, a dog barked, too close for comfort. Rhona could make out the house, grey in the moonlight, through a narrow gate in the wall. A light went off in an upstairs room. Her heart thudded in her chest.

If I was minted, and I lived in that house, and I'd kidnapped a unicorn, and she was havin' a wean, I'd want her nearby, somewhere safe and private and quiet… like that big back garden.

She crept towards the garden gate, crouched low and peered through the bars. The moon's pale light made the lawns look liquid. It shone on a large wooden shed, tucked away in the corner of the garden, half hidden by the drooping branches of a Kilmarnock willow. She looked behind, could see Lewis's shadowy shape and bouncing torch beam as he trudged through the trees towards her.

He might no' like this plan, she thought. *He might no' like it one bit.*

The gate was locked, so she climbed over it, trying to avoid the fancy wrought-iron scrollwork, which snagged at her clothes. The crunching noise her boots made when she landed on the gravel path seemed far too loud. For a moment she stood, heart thumping, on the edge of the huge expanse of lawn, staring at the house, waiting for the dogs to begin a frenzy of barking.

When nobody reacted to her presence, she crept across the grass towards the shed, skirting a stack of hay bales piled in front. Rhona wrinkled her nose. The building had been recently painted with wood preserver, and it reeked. But there was another smell she recognised. She remembered Mr D teasing Ellie, the evening they'd arrived at the Centre. They'd gone out for a walk and had passed a herd of Highland cows.

"Aw, what's that stink?" Ellie had wailed, holding her nose and screwing up her face. "That's pure mingin'!"

Mr D had roared with laughter. "Breathe in that lovely, healthy scent! It's a lot better for your lungs than petrol fumes and pollution. Fresh country air mixed with cow dung."

It was the same smell, Rhona was sure of it. There was definitely an animal in that shed.

Cautiously, she peered over the open half-door.

Shafts of silver moonlight glimmered on the walls and on the floor of the shed's interior, danced over rough-hewn wood walls and a pile of soft straw bedding. Rhona didn't blink, didn't rub at her eyes.

"Oh, jeez," she breathed. The tiny hairs on the back of her neck rose as the animal stirred and gazed up with liquid violet eyes. Moonlight sparkled on her shimmering white coat, her translucent silvery mane. Her spiralled horn glistened with a mother-of-pearl sheen.

There was no doubt, no chance it could be anything else. Rhona was face to face with a beautiful unicorn.

21

Lewis

Lewis hurried after Rhona, following the crunch of her boots on dead leaves. But then the sounds stopped. He switched off his torch because, although it was invisible behind the high wall, he knew the main house was close by. As he passed a gate, his heart stopped.

Rhona was in the garden, her ridiculous white jacket glowing like a beacon.

He peered through the bars and saw her in front of a shed, peering over a stable door. "Rhona? What the heck are you doing?"

She turned, her face pale as the moon, and put a warning finger to her lips. "Shhh! Climb over, quick."

Somewhere in the house, a dog barked.

As Lewis clambered over the garden gate, his heart banged in his ribcage. Why had Rhona put herself so close to harm's way? Was there a unicorn in that shed? Because if there was, he should be running over there, dragging Rhona away from that doorway before she was attacked. He knew how fierce they could be. She was in terrible danger, but for some reason she seemed perfectly calm.

"Come an' see! It's the most amazing thing ever."

"Rhona, you need to be careful. Step back."

Rhona didn't turn round. "Come closer."

He did as he was told, leaned in so that he could get a better view, and then gasped and drew back, awestruck.

Rhona turned to him and laughed. "I've never seen anyone's jaw actually drop before."

He leaned in again, blinking in amazement. "Oh, wow. Rhona, look at her! She's incredible."

"Isn't she stunning?" Rhona whispered. "I wish my hair was as shiny and silky as her mane. She could be in a shampoo advert."

They watched as the unicorn struggled to her feet and walked to a water trough. She was very beautiful, thought Lewis, but she was extremely overweight and she was making odd, grunting noises.

"What's wrong with her?" he asked. "Do you think she's wounded?"

"No, you big daftie. Look at her belly. It's massive. She sounds as though she's about ready to give birth."

Lewis's eyes widened. "What? She's going to have the baby? We need to get help!"

"Who do you suggest we call?" Rhona's voice dripped sarcasm. "Should we run and get the neighbours? What about Ailsa McAllister? She could bring her shotgun and shoot the unicorn in the neck, then saw off her horn. And then make sure we keep quiet about what we've seen by shooting us too."

"I was thinking along the lines of an emergency vet, you eejit. The unicorn's life might be in danger."

"We haven't got mobiles here though, have we? And her life *is* in danger. Look at that chain round her leg. She's trapped in a shed, kidnapped by people who are only interested in how much money she'll make them."

Lewis clicked his tongue with frustration. "Why did Mr Deacon insist on no electronic devices? It's completely irrational. People need mobiles to function."

"It won't have been up to Mr Deacon," said Rhona. "It'll have been the head teacher's or the Outdoor Centre's decision. And it makes sense, cos Ellie would have been calling her dad every single night. She's dead homesick."

"You always take Mr Deacon's side. He's not that wonderful, you know."

Rhona ignored him, as she often did when she thought

he was wrong but couldn't be bothered to argue. She kept her eyes on the unicorn.

"I don't think the birth's going to happen quite yet," she said. "She seems settled enough."

Lewis looked at the unicorn's heaving flanks and didn't feel totally convinced. "Since when did you become an expert on unicorn births?"

"I'm not, you bampot. But I was in class the day they showed us the video of the lamb being born, and I was paying attention, not sitting at the back of the room with my hands over my eyes."

Lewis shuddered at the memory. "There was a lot of gunky stuff. It was gross."

The unicorn turned, fixed him with those deep violet eyes, as if she'd understood every word he'd said, and he felt himself blushing, mortified. He started gabbling, trying to make up for his rudeness.

"You can see why unicorns are a symbol of purity and grace. She's so beautiful."

"Do you think she'd mind if I went in?" Without waiting to hear Lewis's opinion, Rhona unlatched the bottom half of the door and stepped into the shed.

"I wouldn't..." gulped Lewis, but Rhona wasn't paying him any attention.

Cautiously, she crept closer to the panting unicorn and crouched low. Gently, she extended one hand and stroked the animal's silken mane. The unicorn didn't seem to mind Rhona's presence. In fact, she seemed comforted by her touch, and closed her eyes.

Lewis's shoulders relaxed. Rhona turned and looked at him, tears sparkling in her eyes.

"We need to get her out of here."

"We have to—" he began.

In the house, the dog barked again. The unicorn's head jerked up, nearly knocking Rhona backwards. Her upper lip curled and she breathed heavily, sniffing the air. Her ears flicked back and forth. Rhona scrambled to her feet.

"Lewis, someone's coming."

"Get out! Move, quick!"

Feet slipping on wet straw, Rhona raced out of the shed. Lewis slammed the bolt. They scurried behind the pile of hay bales, partially covered by a tarpaulin. Lewis pulled it over their heads. If only they'd had the sense, he thought, to wear dark colours as camouflage. His stupid orange jacket even had reflective strips on the arms.

A beam of yellow light swept over the front of the shed, like a searchlight across a prison yard. For a terrifying moment they both thought they'd been caught. Rhona gasped and Lewis took her outstretched hand, finding strength in its warmth. Two black shadows loomed over the hay bales. Rhona's grip got bone-crushingly tight. He waited, muscles taut, for the dogs to sniff them out.

"I don't know why you made me leave Morag and Flo in the house," grumbled Ailsa. "Something spooked them. They don't usually bark at night."

Lewis relaxed a little. If the dogs weren't there, all they had to do was stay quiet and wait it out.

"The dogs fluster the unicorn, my dear, you know that." Lewis recognised the Laird's kindly voice. "We don't want her upset, not in her condition."

"A fat lot of good either of them would be against a burglar, anyway. More than likely they'd lick them to death. I did suggest you get proper guard dogs. I'm sure I could acquire a couple of Dobermanns or Rottweillers to patrol the grounds at night."

"Heavens, no. What if one of them was to bite one of our visitors?"

He seemed such a kindly old gent, thought Lewis. The old man could have no idea what his niece was like.

Lewis crawled forward, the tarpaulin draped over his shoulders, and peered round the hay bales. He watched the two figures look over the half-door, just as he and Rhona had done. In the torchlight the old man's heavily lined face looked less benign, more goblin than cheery gnome. His eyes looked wet, as if he'd been crying. Ailsa McAllister was holding the torch.

"She's still here. I worried you for nothing. Sorry, Uncle. But I'm a nervous wreck after all these escapes!"

The old man's voice was thick with tears. "I can hardly believe what has happened. The danger we have put these animals in by allowing them to escape! At least our project hasn't been a complete disaster. The mare looks ready to foal. In the next few days, I would guess." He gave a horrified gasp. "Why has she been chained?"

"It's only until I've fitted better locks on the shed. After the mass escape, we can't be too careful. I'll sort everything out tomorrow."

The old man gave a heavy sigh. "A single birth hardly mitigates the disaster of losing the others. Do you think there's any chance one or two are still on the estate? Perhaps that's what spooked the dogs. Have you looked everywhere?"

"I've searched everywhere, Uncle Donald. We don't know exactly when they escaped, but by the time Alex got to the stockade, it was too late. They were long gone. At least, that's what he tells me. I've been all over the moor this afternoon. It's as if they've disappeared from the face of the earth. Maybe unicorns have got magical powers, after all."

Lewis cringed at her sarcastic tone. How could she look at that unicorn she'd captured and not see that it shimmered with magic?

"I wouldn't speak about magic in that mocking way, Ailsa," chided the Laird. "There's definitely something extra special about these creatures. Hopefully they've all made it safely back to Whindfall Forest."

He sighed, and cleared his throat. "To be honest, my dear, since you told me the bad news I've had second thoughts about the programme. I've been doing further research on the island location you suggested and I don't feel it's remote enough. We cannot risk the general public finding out that unicorns exist. It would be dangerous for the animals. Look at the black rhino, the mountain gorilla, the Malayan tiger, all on the verge of extinction, thanks to humans."

"You can't be serious!"

"I'm entirely serious. As a matter of fact, I'm beginning to think we should have left the unicorns well alone. After all, they've survived at Whindfall successfully for hundreds of years."

"Yes, but Uncle, their numbers are low and they're all in one place. If the forest goes, so do the unicorns. Without our breeding programme, they could be extinct within ten years!"

"I shared your initial enthusiasm for the breeding project, Ailsa, and I really thought we were doing the right thing, but let's face it, the whole thing has been a disaster. When the foal is born we shall return the mare and her baby to the forest. I hate to let you down like this, my dear, as I know how hard you've worked, but it has to end."

There was a long, strained silence.

"You can't mean that, Uncle! We can't just let them go! If you don't like the idea of releasing unicorns on to the island, then why don't we consider forming a permanent herd at Langcroft? The unicorns would be an amazing tourist attraction. I can go back to Whindfall, collect some more. Our financial troubles would be over."

"This project was not about making money, my dear." There was a slight rebuke in the Laird's voice. "It was all for the benefit of the unicorns."

"Yes, but—"

"There are no buts." The old man's voice was firm. "Our mission was to provide a safe environment in which these creatures could breed and, ultimately, to return them to the wild. Both Alex and I have come to the decision that the plan is flawed, and, after all, it is Alex who will have the long-term responsibility. I'm sorry my dear, but it's over. That little foal will be our legacy. We shall name it Langcroft."

There was another long silence, broken by Ailsa's voice, unexpectedly brisk and upbeat.

"Of course, Uncle. You're the boss. But look, you're shivering! Go back up to the house. It's really late and we've both got lots to do tomorrow, preparing for the birth."

"Yes, you're right. I'm exhausted. I'm getting too old

for the burden of managing this estate. What would I do without you and Alex?"

The old man walked across the lawn. Ailsa stood, staring into the shed.

"Maybe we should go back?" Lewis whispered.

"Not yet." There was a stubborn note in Rhona's voice.

"Rhona, the Laird just said he's going to let the mare and her foal go free. We don't need to do anything more."

"I don't trust that lassie as far as I could throw her."

Lewis gripped Rhona's arm. Ailsa was talking to herself, her voice an angry hiss.

"So you and Alex have come to a decision, have you? And neither of you thought to ask me? So typical."

There was a short silence, then Lewis heard the metallic click of the bolt. The tall figure of Ailsa stepped forward into the shed.

The unicorn's ears went back until they were almost flat against her head. The mare struggled to get to her feet. She shook her head violently, and her tail swished to and fro. Her eyes rolled back in her head and she squealed, a high, bloodcurdling sound.

"What's happening?" whispered Rhona, but Lewis couldn't answer. His heart was pounding.

"Shut up, you stupid beast." Ailsa's voice was cold as winter. "If my uncle thinks I'm going to let a fortune slip through my fingers, he's a bigger idiot than Alex.

I'm going to remove your horn, and the foal's. I can tell them you died giving birth. Terribly sad, but these things happen."

Horrified, Lewis leaned further forward. He knocked against a rake and it thudded to the ground. Ailsa spun round.

At that moment, the unicorn kicked out with her back legs. Her huge hooves crashed against the walls of the shed. Then she reared, coming down hard on the trailing chain. Ailsa raised her arms above her head, trying to protect herself from the unicorn's flailing hooves. Caught between the unicorn and the side wall, she dropped her torch. It crashed onto the floor and went out.

"We need to get out of here while it's dark. Let's go," Lewis whispered.

He and Rhona shrugged off the tarpaulin and crept away from the shed, towards the gate. They clambered over and started to run as they reached the shelter of the trees. Behind him, Lewis heard a series of thuds, loud curses and the unicorn's furious snorts.

22

Lewis

Despite the night's chill, Lewis felt clammy, his neck sticky with sweat, muscles knotted. Ailsa had her gun with her: at any moment, bullets could start whizzing past their heads.

A murder of crows rose from their treetop nests into the air, cawing. Lewis and Rhona ran through the woods at the back of the house, pushing their way through a tangle of branches, slithering on damp leaf mould.

Then Rhona stopped dead and leaned against an ivy-covered wall, panting for breath. "Lewis, what if Ailsa kills her?"

Lewis shivered. "The unicorn went crazy, didn't she? It was terrifying."

"She didn't go crazy. She was only trying to protect herself and her baby." Rhona clutched at his arm. "Or maybe she was trying to distract Ailsa, and give us a chance to get away. How can we help her?"

"We could tell the police," he said, but there was doubt in his voice.

"We'd have to talk them into checking out the Laird's grounds," said Rhona. "And I don't fancy our chances of that, do you? We've no chance against that woman. She's sneaky as a snake."

"She is, isn't she?" Lewis switched on his torch. The beam caught a door in the wall just as it swung silently open. He jumped in fright, convinced Ailsa had ambushed them, but nobody leapt through the door. A frog croaked, and when he peered through the doorway, he could see stars reflected in a lily pond.

"It's the walled garden," he whispered. "We'll be safe in there."

Rhona didn't argue. She followed him inside and quietly they shut the door.

Exhausted, they flopped down on a stone bench, breathed in the cool air and the heavy scent of roses, feeling the garden's dreamlike stillness. The moon illuminated the garden with its ghost-pale light, silvering the gravel paths, making the white flowers glow. The sculptures stood like sentinels, and the only sounds were the trickle of water from a fountain and the frog's low croak. Lewis didn't quite understand why this garden felt so safe.

A shaft of moonlight glinted on the little unicorn statue in the corner of the garden and cast a shadow on the grass.

"The unicorn statue must be of Dubhar, the unicorn in Alex's story," breathed Rhona. "It has to be! His name means dark shadow."

She walked slowly over, and started rubbing at the plaque with her jacket sleeve.

Lewis shook his head. "Even if you find the inscription, it's not light enough to read."

"Wrong again, pal. Come and look."

He blinked in astonishment, struggling to believe what he was seeing. Each word on the plaque shimmered like mercury. Voice shaking, Lewis read the inscription aloud.

> Whindfall's calling Sneachda home
> The forest's where she needs to be
> But know she cannot go alone
> The Guardians must set her free.

"I guess Sneachda is the mare's name," he said. "But who the heck are the Guardians?"

Rhona snorted, as if he'd said something even more stupid than usual. "Who rescued the unicorns from the stockade? Who came here to try and save Sneachda?

We did, didn't we? We must be the Guardians. But we're running away. We're a big fail."

As Lewis stared at the inscription, the letters melted into a silvery blob, which faded to grey.

"Let's do it." His voice sounded over-loud.

"Do what?"

"We need go and get the unicorn and take her back to Whindfall Forest. And we need to do it tonight. By tomorrow night, we'll be back in Glasgow. It'll be too late to save her and the baby."

Rhona's eyes shone like stars. "OK. How?"

"Don't ask me for the details. I haven't worked those out yet. But I'm going to do it. Are you with me?"

"Well, the inscription said Guardians, plural, didn't it?"

"You're right though. We're hopeless Guardians. We left Ailsa with Sneachda."

Rhona shivered. "If Sneachda's dead," she whispered, "the baby's dead too."

It was a terrible, unbearable thought.

"She isn't dead. I know she's not."

Lewis was gritty-eyed with exhaustion. But for some reason he felt more confident than he had earlier.

As they left the walled garden, clouds scudded across the moon and a smirry rain began to fall, drizzling against their jackets and running in thin rivulets down their faces. Creeping through the woodland, jumping at every cracking twig, the confidence Lewis had felt began to ebb away and was replaced by a gnawing ache. What if they found another dead unicorn? How could he face that? The first had been terrible enough.

As they climbed the garden gate and crept over to the shed, he could see that the door was shut, fastened by another padlock. Ailsa was gone.

Rhona gave the chain a sharp tug. "We can't get in unless we steal the key."

Lewis groaned. "Trespassing, housebreaking, unicorn theft... How many years in jail do you think we'll get?"

"They'll have to catch us first, won't they? But maybe we don't need to housebreak... Switch on your torch for a sec."

The beam swept the ground, flickering over the stack of hay bales, a pitchfork, the rake, a bucket.

Rhona pointed a finger. "Bet the key's under that bucket."

She pushed it over. In the torchlight, a key ring glinted on the grass. Rhona lifted it and jingled the keys in the air, grinning triumphantly.

"How did you know that would be there?" Lewis asked.

She shrugged. "It's what people do, Lewis. I hide my door key under the mat. Don't tell anyone, especially not Kyle. His big brother's a thieving git."

She picked up the keyring to unfasten the padlock.

23

Rhona

Hardly daring to breathe, Rhona leant over the half door and looked into the shed. The unicorn was sprawled on the straw, but her head was upright, her spiralled horn still intact. She was watching them, eyes wary, but alive and well, the crushed chain lying in pieces at her hooves. Tears of relief slid down Rhona's cheeks.

She's no' deid. We're in time.

Cautiously, Rhona unlatched the bottom door and stepped inside. She reached out a tentative hand and stroked the unicorn's long mane, while Lewis stayed at the doorway.

"What now?" he asked. "We can't just let her loose, Rhona. She's not with the rest of the herd. What if she gets lost on the moor?"

The unicorn got to her feet. Rhona put a hand

gently on her muzzle. The mare bowed her head and went very still. They stood like that for a moment, and then Rhona turned to Lewis.

"I'm sure she wants us to set her free."

"How do you know that? Since when have you learned to speak unicorn?"

Rhona shrugged. "I can just sense it. You need to go with her. She might need help on the way. Her baby will be born soon."

"I'm not a vet! What help can I be?"

Rhona gave him her 'stop being a numpty' glare.

"But I've no idea how to get to Whindfall Forest!" he protested. "It's a crazy plan."

"No, it isn't. It's sensible. And she knows the way home, she's no' daft."

"I'm not leaving you here. You have to come too."

"It's no' fair to ask her to carry two people. I'm going to chap at the door of that house and let the Laird know exactly what his precious niece is up to."

Lewis shook his head vehemently. "No way. Far too dangerous. I'm not going without you. End of."

Rhona could tell that his protests about how he couldn't leave her behind weren't him being brave. She knew he was afraid to do this on his own.

"Lewis, you can do this. I'm scared too. But we've come all this way to rescue the unicorn. We can't back out now."

The unicorn seemed to lose patience with them. She leant forward and nudged Lewis with her long muzzle. Rhona grinned.

"You'd better do what she wants. She might stab you."

He nodded, took a deep, gulping breath, opened the bucket, upended it and used it to help him scramble onto the unicorn's broad back. Leaning down, he put his hand out to Rhona. "I can do this alone. But I'd rather you were with me."

Rhona shook her head. "Don't you know how lucky you are? How many people in history have ridden on a unicorn? This could be an actual first."

He gave her a weak smile. "What should I say? 'Giddy up' seems totally disrespectful."

"Just ask nicely. I'll go and unlock the garden gate. I think this other key should do the trick." She held up the key ring and grinned.

Lewis leaned forward, close to the unicorn's left ear. "Excuse me, ma'am, but it's time to go."

The unicorn tossed her head so that her mane rippled like silk. She blew through her nostrils and set off into the night, hooves high.

24

Lewis

As soon as the unicorn began to move, Lewis panicked, overwhelmed by dizziness. The unicorn was taller than any horse he'd ever ridden, though, to be honest, he'd only ridden one in his entire life, on a pony trek on Ardrossan Beach when he was six.

He was a long, long way from the ground. If he fell, he'd be crushed by her hooves, he'd break his neck, he'd…

The unicorn broke into a trot and Lewis gave up on thought. He focused on listening to the beat of her hooves on the ground while gripping her mane so tightly his fingertips whitened. She started to move across the garden towards Rhona, who'd run to the gate and was fiddling with the padlock. Lewis moaned, consumed by fear, as the gate swung open. Rhona raced off, swallowed up by the darkness as she headed towards the big house.

The unicorn moved through the garden gate and slowed down, picking her way delicately through the thick undergrowth. Lewis leaned forward, afraid he'd be decapitated by an overhanging branch or garrotted by trailing vines. A strange sense of calm settled over him. The unicorn knew exactly what she was doing. All he had to do was hold tight.

"You're doing brilliantly," he whispered. "You can do this."

The unicorn twitched her ears, as if she liked the sound of his voice.

He remembered that bleak night, lost on the moor, when the stallion had seemed to be his enemy. He'd been so convinced in those terrible, panicked moments that it had been coming straight for him, but now he knew for certain he hadn't been the target of the unicorn's rage. He thought of the odd circular dent in the side of the Land Rover. Ailsa must have been somewhere near him that night. He hoped she'd got the fright of her life when the unicorn's horn smacked against the car door.

Lewis shook his head, trying to clear his thoughts.

He was starting to get worried about the time this unicorn was taking, negotiating the woodland. But as she broke from the cover of the trees, he felt a twinge of excitement. They were on their way to freedom, he and Sneachda. The unicorn's hooves clattered as she broke into a trot. Behind them, raindrops rippled the black waters of the loch. Soon they'd be out on the moor, heading for the forest. Soon the unicorn would be free again. They were almost at the main gates... the padlocked gates.

He'd forgotten... he'd forgotten that Ailsa had locked the main gates. They had no key for those.

Panic gripped Lewis's chest, tightened his throat. Without any warning, the unicorn stopped dead and he lunged forward. He'd have gone head first if he hadn't been grasping Sneachda's mane so tightly.

Legs splayed, the unicorn leant right back. Her ears swivelled back and forth; her eyes darted. Lewis felt the trembling in her body, could sense her fear. As he stared, a shadowy figure stepped out from behind a bush and activated a security light.

"Ailsa," he breathed.

Ailsa took another step forward, into the pool of bright light. The shotgun was at her shoulder, aimed right at the unicorn's head. Her features were twisted with rage.

"You're trespassing on private property. Get down. Now!" There was an ominous click as she cocked the gun. "Right now, or I'll have to shoot you. Please don't think I won't. Your silly friend tried to stop me getting in my car and I dealt with her. This is a huge estate. There's a deep loch, a stone quarry, peat bogs. Your bodies will never be found. Your parents will think you've died on the moor. Your teachers will be blamed for not keeping a better eye on you. It won't be news for long."

Lewis shook his head, trying to ignore the hammering in his heart. He didn't doubt she was capable of murder. But would she really take the risk of killing them here, when the Laird was nearby?

"I don't believe you. You wouldn't dare. The Laird would know what you've done. Let us past. Sneachda, go!"

The ground seemed to topple away. Lewis held tight. Sneachda was rising up onto her hind legs, sharp hooves flailing. Eyes wide with terror, Ailsa leapt back and the gun went off, loud as thunder.

Sneachda veered away from the gates and they cantered past the oak tree he and Rhona had climbed to get in. The unicorn reached a crumbling section of wall and her huge hooves struck against it: once, twice, three times. Part of the stonework collapsed, toppled onto the grass verge beyond. Sneachda jumped the remains of the wall, clumsy because of her bulk. Her hooves clashed against the stonework, sending sparks flying into the night sky.

But she'd done it. They were over the wall.

Lewis clung on, knuckles white, waiting for a bullet in his back. His throat was raw and the blood was pounding in his head. He tried to think.

Should I fling myself off, get back over the wall and find out what's happened to Rhona? Or would I be better running to the Centre for help? If I go back, Ailsa's there. How can I help Rhona if she shoots me too? What would Rhona want?

The unicorn's heavy hooves clattered on the tarmac. She galloped onto the main road, straight along the white line, oblivious to any road rules or possible traffic. Lewis tried to steady his breathing, as he had when he was stuck in the bog. That incident seemed trivial now, a fuss about nothing. He'd been ankle-deep; now he was up to his neck in trouble.

Think… If I jump off, the chances are I'll break a leg. I'll be no use to Rhona whatsoever, crawling along the main road in the dark. If I only had my phone I could dial 999. Cos if Rhona's lying injured, Ailsa will let her bleed to death, no question.

What if Rhona's already dead?

Without warning, the unicorn swerved to the right, across the road and onto the moor. Lewis's body was flung sideways and he grabbed her mane, dragging himself upright. As he struggled, a thought flickered through his brain. He didn't know if it was his or if he was hearing someone else's voice.

This mustn't be for nothing.

Squeezing his eyes shut, he held on.

He felt he'd been awake all night, but when he checked

his watch the sickly green numbers showed 2:45. Whindfall was about five miles from the Outdoor Centre. Langcroft was two miles from the Centre. He tried to work out the maths, but numbers weren't his strong point at the best of times. According to the second-most-read book on his shelf, *The Wonderful World of Animals,* a galloping horse travels at forty kilometres an hour. That meant… he didn't have a clue what it meant. Exhaustion and cold were creeping into his limbs. His hands felt numb. He didn't know how much longer he could keep going.

And then he heard it: a car, its engine vrooming. The sounds travelled through the dark: the squeak of dodgy suspension, the squeal of tyres. He twisted round and saw the Land Rover, only a hundred metres behind them. The headlights were blinding and he couldn't make out who was at the wheel. There was a deafening bang. A bullet whizzed past his ear.

It's Ailsa. She's found us. We're done for. I'm sorry, Rhona. I'm so sorry.

The Land Rover was gaining ground, gears crunching as it dragged itself up the hillside, churning up mud. Its headlights picked out the unicorn, however desperately she dodged. And she was flagging badly: her coat was slicked with sweat and her hooves stumbled and slipped on the damp grass and scattered rocks. Lewis strained to see, but it was pitch-dark ahead.

Lewis could no longer tell if the pounding sound was his heart or the unicorn's hooves. The Land Rover was almost at their heels. It swerved to the side. Another shot ran out, thunderously loud. The unicorn's whole body shuddered, and her head jerked back as the bullet whizzed past them, thwacked into something solid. Lewis leaned even further forward, so his head was on the unicorn's neck.

"Keep going," he whispered. "You'll soon be home."

He had no idea if this was the truth, but he could tell she was at the end of her tether, needing some hope.

The vehicle swerved again, aiming straight for them. Its headlights lit up the way and Lewis let out the breath he'd been holding. His shoulders sagged with relief. There was a forest ahead, thick and dark. Its perimeter was guarded by a battalion of tall Scots pines.

"We've made it. She can't follow us in there."

With a final surge of energy, the unicorn galloped towards the trees. As she reached them, it was as if the tree trunks drew back to let her enter, then reformed into a bristling, impenetrable line. Behind them Lewis heard a screech of brakes, a piercing, furious scream.

Ailsa wouldn't give up. He was sure of it. She'd follow them on foot, shotgun in hand. But it was pitch-black in the forest. She wouldn't have the car lights to guide her. And the unicorn seemed to know exactly which way she was heading. She picked her way delicately over tree roots, rotting fungi and dead leaves. Steam billowed from her nostrils and her coat felt damp with sweat, but she held her head high. This was Whindfall Forest, and she'd come home.

Despite his fear and exhaustion, Lewis felt proud. He'd fulfilled his promise to the stallion. He'd brought Sneachda safely home. But he was a long, long way from his own home. And his best friend was missing. If Alex's story was true, this forest was cursed: was it a danger to all humans or only to those who meant to harm the unicorns? Lewis knew he had to leave. He'd got the unicorn to Whindfall, and now he had to find Rhona.

25

Lewis

It was as if Sneachda could hear Lewis's thoughts. The unicorn stopped dead. He slid off her back and tumbled to the ground, onto a carpet of soggy leaves. As Sneachda disappeared into the trees, he rummaged in his pockets for his torch.

There was a large, dark shape moving among the trees. "Sneachda?" he whispered.

A deep silence fell, as though each forest creature had pricked up its ears and was waiting for him to speak again. He clamped his mouth shut and slowly turned, moving the torch in a wide arc. Wherever the beam lit, another large shape flashed past in the shadows. In the distance he could hear a low, steady drumming of hooves. It seemed the whole forest was alive. He wasn't alone at all. He was surrounded.

Lewis pressed his back against a tree, the rough bark scraping his jacket. Standing perfectly still, torch beam focused on one spot, he listened for the sound of Ailsa's footsteps, the click of a trigger. He was being watched.

He raised the torch higher and the beam shone on a gleaming, spiralled pewter horn, a grey silk mane.

"Liath? It's Liath, isn't it?"

The unicorn tossed its head and slipped away into the darkness.

"Wait! Liath, please wait!"

Lewis tried to follow, tripping over dead logs, crashing into dense thickets, clumsy in the torchlight. As he stumbled, the light kept flickering. Then it died.

"I had a dodgy battery too, Rhona," he muttered, stuffing the torch back in his pocket, his stomach clenching in fear at the thought of being lost in this dark, spooky forest.

But there was a little moonlight now, filtering through the trees, silvering the leaves, and as his eyes got used to it, the forest became less terrifying. The small creatures whose scurrying feet had freaked him out were tiny wood mice and voles, foraging for food. The eerie screeches above came from a beautiful, pale-feathered barn owl, eyeing him from the treetops. The large silver-grey shadows that flashed past, just out of focus, were unicorns.

The ground became stonier underfoot. He reached

an outcrop with trailing ivy and lush ferns, the wet rocks glistening in moonlight. A stream of glittering water trickled over lichen-stained stones before cascading over the rock face and splashing into a pool. A unicorn trotted from the cover of the trees, bent its head and started to drink from the pool.

Lewis took off his filthy glasses and rubbed them on his sleeve, wanting a clearer view. This forest *was* magical, and he wished Rhona was with him. But something startled the unicorn. She shook her silver mane, sending droplets of water flying like tiny shooting stars, and galloped off into the trees.

Behind him, a twig snapped.

"I've had more than enough of this. It ends here."

He whirled round, lifted his hand to shield his eyes, dazzled by the light. When his vision cleared, he saw Ailsa, carrying a torch in one hand and dragging something along behind her with the other. Her shotgun was slung over her back. As she swung her left arm, the thing she was dragging pitched forward into the pool, then emerged, spluttering and coughing.

Lewis recognised the jacket first. Relief made his knees buckle and he grabbed a rock for support.

"Rhona! You're not dead!"

Ailsa swung her torch so the beam hit him again, full in the face. "She's not dead… yet."

Rhona picked herself up, swept a hand through her wet hair. "Course I'm no' deid. Why would I be? Though I've been thrown into the back of a pick-up, kidnapped and nearly drowned, which are serious criminal offences, by the way, hen. You're going to be in such bother when I tell the polis."

Lewis stood dumbly, staring at his friend. He was so glad to see her.

"I… I thought you'd been shot," he stammered. "I thought you'd been killed."

"I told you, I'm fine. Where's Sneachda? The poor beast must be shattered."

He saw her looking around for the unicorn, eyes raking the darkness.

"She's gone," he whispered.

Ailsa gave a shriek of frustration. "Of course she's gone! What did you expect, that she'd hang around to say thank you? All that work, all the time it took to trap those beasts, and you two brats have ruined everything."

"Yeah, that was the plan. Sneachda will be miles away now. Lewis is a flamin' hero."

Lewis was about to point out that he was no such thing, and that provoking Ailsa was a terrible idea, when Rhona kicked out with her heavy boot and sent Ailsa's torch spinning through the air. It smacked against a pine tree. His world went dark.

Rhona grabbed his hand. "Run, Lewis!"

And they ran, out of the clearing, back into the dense forest, stumbling over tree roots, scattering leaves. As he charged through the darkness, Lewis was again aware of shadowy shapes among the trees, thudding hooves, the occasional whinny.

Rhona slowed to a jog, panting for breath. "I think I'm goin' to spew... I can't run another step... I'm dying... Lewis, stop a moment."

He didn't want to stop. Adrenalin was coursing through him. But he couldn't go without Rhona.

So he stopped, stood still, listened.

Unicorns were close by. He could hear the soft thump of hooves, snorting breaths.

Moonlight filtered through the slender branches of birch trees and silvered the grey coat of a unicorn only a few metres away. The animal's head was held high, nostrils quivering as it sniffed the air. Then it moved off at a brisk trot.

Lewis brought out his torch, gave it a hard shake. The beam flickered, became a faint, but steady glow. He spun round, shining the torch on bushes and trees, searching for signs of life until the beam rested on a tall pine.

At its base lay Sneachda, and she wasn't alone.

Her body was curled protectively round a small, dark shape. Lewis's torch beam glinted on the foal's silk coat, its closed eyes and its tiny spiralled horn. His stomach knotted as he realised the baby wasn't moving.

Sneachda was licking the foal with her long tongue.

"What's wrong with it?" The words caught in Lewis's throat, choked him. Was the foal not going to live?

But as they watched, the mare arched her neck and bent her head. The tip of her iridescent horn touched the foal's body, once, twice, three times. For a long moment, the baby didn't respond; but then it gave a little cough, opened its eyes and kicked its skinny legs.

"Aw, man," said Lewis, tears stinging his eyes. "Sneachda's baby's fine."

Rhona crouched down beside him. "Well spotted, Lewis. Good observational skills. You get ten out of ten this time."

Her words were as snarky as ever, but Lewis heard the tremor in her voice, and knew she'd been scared too.

The baby's mother looked up at them and seemed to relax. She lowered her long lashes, licked the baby with her massive tongue. The baby curled beside its mother, nuzzling, looking for milk.

Rhona spoke to the unicorn directly. "Well done, hen! Congratulations. You've got a beautiful wean there."

The unicorn tossed her head, her mane shimmering in the moonlight.

The baby kicked its spindly legs, made tiny huffing sounds. Then it scrambled up on to its feet, wobbly as Bambi.

Lewis could feel a huge, stupid grin spread across his face. The baby unicorn was the most enchanting little creature he'd ever seen in his life. It wobbled around on its skittery limbs, its silvery coat smooth as silk.

Rhona's grin was enormous too. She was bouncing like a manic wallaby.

"Aw, she's adorable! Would it be OK if I gave her a wee pat?" She was talking to the unicorn.

"Rhona, we need to go," he said. "We need to get out of this forest."

Because somewhere in the darkness, Ailsa was still tracking her prey.

26

Rhona

A male voice called out, and the tiny hairs on Rhona's neck rose. She could hear the heavy tread of boots, the thud getting louder as the person approached. Her eyes darted in all directions, but she knew they were too late to run.

"Who's there?"

Lewis swung his dodgy torch in the direction of the voice and Rhona recognised the tall, gangly figure in jeans and wax jacket coming through the trees towards them.

"It's Alex McAllister," she hissed, standing in front of the unicorn and her foal, arms outstretched protectively. "You'll take them over my deid body!" she roared. "Come one step nearer and I'll… I'll nut you!"

Alex kept coming. As he drew nearer, she could see his face, creased in astonishment. He shone his torch at her, dazzling her.

"What on earth are you kids doing here in the middle of the night?" He pointed at Rhona. "I know you. You were at the storytelling session at the Outdoor Centre. You asked me about the condition that the Winter Queen set, wanted to know what happened to Dubhar."

In her head, Rhona could hear the almost reverential tone Alex had used when describing Dubhar's courage and sacrifice. But could they trust him, when Ailsa was his sister?

Lewis stepped forward. "We could ask you the same question. And we know all about the unicorn project, so there's no point telling us any lies. Rhona and I released the unicorns from the stockade."

It was the second time that night that Rhona had seen someone's jaw drop. Alex's eyes were wide with surprise. Then he chuckled.

"Did you now! Well done, you two. I've been up here all night, checking that they all got back to Whindfall safely, and I'm guessing they have, as this place seems to be teeming with them. It's just as well I mean the unicorns no harm, or I'd be a dead man. But you still haven't explained why *you're* here in the forest."

It wasn't my idea to come here," growled Rhona. "Ailsa kidnapped me. I don't mean to be cheeky, an' I know you two are related, but that lassie's meaner than Cruella De Vil."

In the torchlight, Rhona could see a worried frown settle on Alex's face. "My sister's in the forest? Has she actually entered Whindfall?"

"Yeah, and I hope she's got well lost. We're lookin' after the wean." Rhona stepped aside and Lewis directed his torch beam at Sneachda.

A huge smile spread across Alex's face. "Oh, my goodness, look at that. The foal's a wee beauty. But how did the mare get up here? Did my uncle bring her?"

Rhona and Lewis looked at each other, unsure how far to trust him. Alex scanned their faces, must have seen the doubt in their eyes.

"None of this was my idea, I swear it. Ailsa never told me what she was up to and neither did Uncle Donald. It was only when I came back to Langcroft permanently that Ailsa revealed their plans. I was horrified, believe me."

Lewis snorted. "Not horrified enough. You should have gone to the police."

Alex gave a rueful laugh. "You're forgetting unicorns are considered to be mythical creatures. If I'd told the authorities that they actually exist, the Whindfall unicorns wouldn't have stayed secret for long. The whole world would have come to visit. My uncle and I have talked non-stop about what's best for them. I'm glad I managed to persuade him to abandon the project."

"Yeah, but you didn't talk your sister round, did you?"

Rhona spoke more angrily than she'd intended. "Your uncle might have been going to let the mare go, but Ailsa was planning to steal her horn and the foal's."

"We rescued them all." There was no mistaking the pride in Lewis's voice.

"You've done an excellent job, getting all the unicorns home." There was real respect in Alex's tone. "Whindfall has been the unicorns' refuge for centuries. They're back now and need to be left in peace. We need to get out of their forest."

"Specially Ailsa," said Rhona, remembering Alex's worried look. "You think she's in danger, don't you, because of Beira's curse? Remember the legend, Lewis? *Nobody who enters the forest intending to harm a unicorn will live to see winter.*"

Alex nodded. "Ailsa has never ventured into the forest before. She's never dared."

Behind them, someone hissed like a snake.

"Well I've dared now." Ailsa stepped out of the darkness, her shotgun raised.

27

Lewis

Lewis's insides turned to liquid. He'd thought they'd made it. They even had adult help now. But what good was that against an armed maniac?

"You were pathetically easy to track," she said with a bitter laugh. "And I'm taking that foal back to Langcroft. I've not done all this work for nothing. This isn't one of your stupid fairy tales, Alex. It's real life, something you've never had to bother about. The unicorns were my project and you've ruined it. You and Uncle Donald didn't even bother to consult me about ending it. It makes me sick that you always get your own way."

Alex sighed. "Don't be daft, Ailsa. Can't you see that what you were doing was wrong? The unicorns don't—"

"Oh shut up! I'm sick of listening to you drone on about how special unicorns are! They're just wild animals, like deer. Deer get shot and nobody whines about it, do they? I can shoot unicorns if I want to. Watch me!" She pulled the trigger, firing wildly into the woods.

"Ailsa! Stop it! You'll hurt somebody!" Alex shouted.

Lewis stared through the trees, and he saw them. When he spoke, his voice sounded scratchy with fear, even to himself. "I think we need to leave. Now. Right now." He gestured with his torch.

No matter where the beam fell, it spotlit another unicorn. A massive herd was heading through the trees towards them. The night air drummed with a dark, unpredictable beat.

Something terrible is going to happen.

"Oh jeez," whispered Rhona. "These guys aren't happy."

All around them, huge, majestic unicorns were pawing at the ground, jerking their heads, snorting. Clouds of steam billowed from their nostrils. Some were midnight-black, hardly visible, others grey as shadows or gleaming snow-white in the torchlight. All had huge spiralling horns sharp as spears. As they came nearer, Lewis could feel their anger, radiating like heat.

Alex grabbed him by the shoulders. He took Rhona's hand and they started to run, dodging between the trees. Alex pulled Ailsa along too, but she struggled, determined to get free. Lewis glanced behind. The unicorns weren't charging; they were moving at a steady trot, gaining on them slowly but steadily.

Perhaps they have no intention of attacking. Maybe they're just trying to persuade us to leave them alone.

Alex was puffing at his side, getting slower with every step. Lewis took the lead. Then he saw her: snow-bright Sneachda was trotting ahead, and her baby, already much steadier on her feet, was stepping along at her side.

"This way!" he shouted to the others, and they followed the white unicorn and her foal, guiding them out of Whindfall Forest. The herd followed slowly, making sure the humans left.

They'd reached the forest perimeter, the line of tall Scots pine. Lewis could glimpse the Land Rover, and Alex's Range Rover some distance away. Sneachda stopped, shaking her mane and tossing her head.

At that moment, Ailsa jerked her arm back and pulled away from Alex.

"I'm not going back empty-handed!" she yelled, spitting rage. She ran straight for the baby unicorn.

For a moment, Lewis was paralysed with shock. Then he screamed, "Ailsa, no! Leave the baby alone! Run, Ailsa, run!"

But he was too late. There was nothing any of them could do but stare in horror as Sneachda, the beautiful snow-white unicorn, lowered her head and got ready to charge. Ailsa had almost reached the foal when Sneachda thumped her hooves against the ground and gave a snort of fury. The girl stopped dead, realising what Sneachda was about to do. Spinning round, she started to run for her life, her eyes swivelling frantically as she searched for somewhere to hide.

"Climb a tree!" bawled Alex.

Ailsa must have heard him, because she raced towards a massive beech, but she never reached it. A sudden wind whistled through the trees; high branches creaked. It seemed to Lewis as if the whole forest was closing in on Ailsa and leaving her no escape. In the shadow of the trees, unicorns were stamping their hooves, an ominous drumbeat signalling her doom.

It happened so fast that later Lewis would only remember a blur: a terrible crack, the huge branch breaking off the beech tree, spinning as it fell, the awful thud, and Ailsa's body sprawled, lifeless, on the bracken.

Rhona's hand shot to her mouth. "Oh… oh no."

Lewis stood, slack-jawed, glued to the spot. The white unicorn tossed her mane and whinnied at her baby. The little one walked towards her, head held high, and together they trotted off into the forest. As Lewis gawped, the other unicorns slowly backed off, melting away into the trees, until it was as if he'd imagined they'd been there.

28

Rhona

Rhona sat down on a tree stump, put her head in her hands and sobbed. She'd loathed Ailsa, but seeing her felled by that massive branch was horrible.

Lewis crouched beside her, his face streaked with tears. "Alex has phoned for an air ambulance. He looks shattered."

"Ailsa's death," she whispered. "do you think it was an accident or the curse of Whindfall?"

For a long moment, Lewis stayed silent. When he spoke, it sounded as though he was picking his words with care. "I didn't know anything about a curse. But remember that sign in the forest at Langcroft? 'Beech trees are susceptible to sudden branch drop."

Alex came over, his face ashen. He gestured behind them. "I've rolled the branch and covered her body with a blanket from the car. The air ambulance will be here shortly."

"I'm really sorry, Alex." Rhona stopped, unsure what else to say.

"At least she's at peace now." Alex was weeping and wringing his hands. "I've never known a person so consumed with jealousy and bitterness. It began when Uncle Donald and I went without her on a camping trip, only because she was invited to a friend's sleepover and was moaning she'd miss it. When we picked her up the following day and told her we'd rescued a trapped unicorn, she was furious. She accused us of always leaving her out, and she never forgave either of us."

He was silent for a moment, and then continued, his voice cracking.

"The irony is, Uncle Donald adored Ailsa. When he made me Langcroft's heir, he apologised to me, because he saw the estate as a burden. He didn't want Ailsa to have that responsibility because he thought she was desperate to travel the world. He didn't know the real reasons behind her visit to Africa, and I'll make sure he never finds out. He'll be heartbroken enough."

Alex sighed again, ran a hand over his stubbled chin.

"As for you two, tell nobody what happened here tonight, do you hear me? We need to keep the unicorns' existence a secret, if any good is to come out of tonight's terrible events…"

They both nodded.

"I'll drive you to the main road and then come back and meet the helicopter. I reckon you've been through more than enough for one night."

Rhona shook her head. "I'm no' getting in a car wi' a stranger. No way."

She heard Lewis's quiet groan. He clearly didn't fancy the idea of a five-mile walk. It would be morning by the time they reached the Centre and they'd have a heck of a lot of explaining to do.

When she stood up, her knees almost buckled. "Come on, Lewis. Let's go, before I keel over. I'm shattered."

Morning was coming, fading out the moon's pale glow. When a unicorn grey as a cloud broke from the shelter of the trees and galloped towards them, he'd have been almost invisible against the leaden sky, if it hadn't been for his gleaming pewter horn.

Yelling, Alex dropped his phone, grabbed Lewis, who was nearest to him, and dragged him into the narrow gap between the two cars. "Run, Rhona!"

But Rhona stayed exactly where she was. As the unicorn slowed to a trot and stopped right in front of her, she smiled and lifted a hand in greeting.

"Good to see you again, Liath."

The unicorn's silvery mane swayed, as he lowered his head. He knelt, allowing both children to clamber on to his back.

Alex shook his head in amazement. "Wow. What are you two, unicorn whisperers?"

Rhona grinned. "We're the Guardians of the Wild Unicorns, actually."

Alex nodded, and waved goodbye. "Remember, say nothing."

"Folk would think we were haverin'," said Rhona, wrinkling her nose. "They all think unicorns are made up."

On the ride back to the Outdoor Centre, Lewis half-dozed and Rhona's thoughts spun round in her head.

If the branch hadn't fallen, would Sneachda have charged? Would she have killed Ailsa? After all, she had to protect her baby. It's what parents do.

The sun peeped over the horizon, bathing the moor in a warm apricot glow. Rhona tightened her grip on Lewis's waist and leaned in so he could hear her.

"That baby unicorn's lucky, isn't she? Her mum is always going to be there for her, keeping her safe." She paused. "I'm sorry I got mad at you earlier."

Lewis said nothing. He was clearly struggling to remember, and she couldn't blame him. Everything that had happened before she'd entered Whindfall Forest seemed foggy, distant history.

But Rhona kept going. She'd kept her worries to herself for too long. It was time she dragged them into the light. Maybe Mr D was right and they'd all shrivel up and die.

"I wasn't being fair. You weren't to know. I've never talked about it."

Lewis twisted round, then had to steady himself by grasping Liath's mane. "Oh, yes, I remember now. I compared your mum with my dad… and you got angry. I'm sorry if I offended you. I wasn't trying to be mean. It's just that I've never seen your mum up at the school, so I figured something must be wrong with her."

Rhona couldn't help it. She bristled. "And because Eastgate has its problems, you assumed Mum was an alcoholic or a junkie?"

There was another awkward silence.

"No… yes… maybe. I said sorry, Rhona. So why doesn't she ever come up to school? Why do you never invite me over to yours?"

As soon as he asked, Rhona's words flooded out, a tsunami of pent-up frustration.

"It's too much for her, that's why. Mum's got severe rheumatoid arthritis, plus agoraphobia, so she won't go outside, even on good days. To be honest, the arthritis is easier to cope with. I mean, it isn't easy. It's terrible. Mum's hands are like claws. She's in agony sometimes and she can do virtually nothing for herself. When it's really bad she uses a wheelchair, just to get around in the house."

She stopped for breath, then told the rest. It was a relief

to let it all out, but she didn't feel her worries shrivelling. They were still there, huge and threatening, lying in wait for her when she got home, ready to leap on her as soon as she got through the front door.

"Sometimes it's hard not to get hacked off about the agoraphobia. I used to get so mad when she wouldn't do simple stuff like picking me up from school or getting groceries from the corner shop, but I've got more patient as I've got older. I understand she can't help it and she'd change if she could. But I still want to shake her some days, and then I feel like the worst person in the world."

"You're not, Rhona. It must be really hard for you. Does your mum have people to come in and look after her?"

"She doesn't like other people to see her when she's in a bad way. She's too proud. I'm Mum's main carer."

Lewis whirled round so fast he almost tumbled off the unicorn's back. His eyes looked as startled as if she'd said she was a government spy.

"You're her main carer? But you can't be! You've got school and homework and…"

His voice faded, and Rhona laughed, a small, mirthless laugh.

"I haven't anything else, Lewis. Didn't you ever wonder why I don't go to after-school sports clubs, why I don't often meet up with you at weekends?"

Lewis's voice was tinged with guilt. "I guess I was afraid

your mum would dredge up memories of my dad. I'd convinced myself she'd be slumped on the couch, drinking vodka straight from the bottle. But I never bothered to find out, never tried to get involved. I've been far too busy worrying about myself. I'm a selfish pig."

"You weren't to know. I don't get time to do other stuff, because I'm too busy, cooking and cleaning and looking after my mum." She gave a tiny sigh of frustration. "She needs me. I wouldn't be here on this residential if it wasn't for Mr D. He organised it all for me: the respite care for Mum, the funds, even the clothes. The man's a pure legend."

"I've been a complete fail, haven't I?"

"Och, no. You're the best. Total pain sometimes, but the best."

"Thanks, pal. You're OK too. But I do think you should talk to your mum, see if you can get yourselves some outside help. From a selfish-pig point of view, it'd be nice to see you at weekends."

Rhona stared out at the huge expanse of moorland, surrounded by snow-capped mountains, and let out a huge, sad sigh. She turned and gave Lewis a watery smile.

"The unicorns weren't too proud to ask for help."

"Nope."

"I could talk to Mum, tell her it's too much for me. Have a proper chat with Mr D, see what can be done."

"Yup."

The unicorn slowed to a walking pace and Rhona realised Liath had carried them all the way back. They were approaching the Outdoor Centre.

She slid off the unicorn's back, rubbed her aching legs. "Thanks, Liath. You're a pal."

Liath stood perfectly still, waiting for Lewis, but Rhona could sense the animal's nervousness, his impatience to head back to Whindfall. As soon as Lewis's feet hit the ground, the unicorn shook its mane and veered around, muscles rippling, hooves clashing against the tarmac. Rhona reached out to touch his silken coat for the last time. He galloped off, leaving a single word drifting on the breeze.

Saorsa…

Rhona stood, oblivious to the early morning chill, watching the unicorn as it headed homewards across the moor, hooves pounding, silver mane flying. When Lewis placed his hand on her shoulder, she jumped.

"We need to go," he said. "Let's hope nobody's shut the toilet window."

"They wouldn't be so daft. OK, let's do it. Back to the Toilet of Doom. By the way, I think the baby unicorn's name is Saorsa."

29

Lewis

They crept up to the main building and squeezed through the open toilet window. Rhona exited the toilet first, and Lewis followed two minutes later. He was sneaking down the corridor, shoes in his hand, when a loud voice made him jump like a frog.

"Lewis! What on earth are you up to now?"

He whipped round, barefoot but fully dressed, shoes dangling from his hand. Mr Deacon was standing behind him, hands on hips, glowering. He was wearing striped pyjamas and old men's slippers, so it was hard to take him seriously. Lewis's preprepared lie came as quick and easy as a microwave meal.

"I woke early and I didn't want to disturb anyone, so I got dressed and went into the common room." He pulled the torch from his jacket pocket. "I used this and read some of the old wildlife magazines that were lying around. Did you know this is a good place to spot pine martens? Did you know that fourteen people have been killed by adders in Britain in the last hundred and fifty years? Would you like me to tell you ten fascinating facts about capercaillies?"

Mr Deacon yawned. "You can tell us all over breakfast, Lewis. Get back to your bed, for goodness' sake."

Lewis nodded and slipped into the dormitory. He pulled off his outer clothes, threw himself on the bed and fell instantly asleep.

He could smell Derek's appalling musky deodorant. When he opened his eyes he could see Derek, in Spiderman boxers, spraying deodorant over his equally stinky trainers.

"That reeks," he murmured, still half asleep.

Derek spun round, sprayed a jet of deodorant over Lewis's bed. "There you go. You'll smell better now. What was all that about last night?"

"What do you mean?" Lewis asked, trying to suss him out. Yawning, he pushed off the duvet, swung his legs across and sat on the edge of the bed. When he pulled off his T-shirt, his muscles twanged. Grimacing, he examined the bruises on his skinny calves. There was a large graze on his shoulder and his hand was badly scratched. He looked like he'd been in a fight.

"You sneaked out and didn't come back until it got light. I was dead worried. I didn't know if I should call Mr Deacon. How far did you get this time?"

Derek seemed genuinely interested, but Lewis was still trying to process all that had happened last night.

"I wasn't running away." For some reason, it seemed important for Derek to know that. "I went… I went looking for something I'd lost."

"What was that, then?"

Lewis tapped his nose. "Top secret. If I told you, I'd have to kill you."

Derek grinned, seeming pleased with this answer. He stuffed his deodorant can into an already full case, then peered at Lewis through his thick-lensed varifocals.

"You don't look too good. Just as well we're going home."

We're going home.

Lewis didn't think he'd ever heard three lovelier words. He smiled at Derek, feeling a twinge of guilt. Derek always tried to be friends and he'd always looked down on him. Let's face it: Lewis had sneered at him. And Derek was nice. He'd been worried about Lewis.

Lewis dragged himself out of bed. He looked down at his tangled sheets, his rumpled duvet. Every other bed was already crisply made. Maybe he should do the same, just to get peace.

Dizzy with tiredness, he got up and smoothed

his duvet. From the other side of the room, Tariq chucked a sock at him.

"Nice one, Lewis. We've definitely won this. I heard the girls' dorm's a tip."

It felt like acceptance.

After breakfast, Scott and Max gave a farewell speech, during which Flora sat in floods of tears, sniffing loudly and declaring herself heartbroken.

"What's she like?" grumbled Rhona. "Every ruddy day's a drama starring Flora."

Lewis sighed, flicked his hair out of his eyes. Maybe he should get it cut, stop hiding behind his fringe. Or maybe he should dye it purple, something a bit more standout than black.

"It feels weird to be going home, for everything to just go back to normal," Lewis said. "I mean, I'm glad it's over and that the unicorns are safe. And I'll be really glad to be back in my own bed. But life's going to feel a bit flat."

"Yup. Eastgate's definitely a unicorn-free zone. We're going back to boring old normal."

Rhona's eyes looked sad, and Lewis remembered that her 'normal' was caring for her mum. It was hard to imagine what that would be like: coming home from school to housework, having to make his own dinner and clean up afterwards. It had never even crossed his mind to do that in his own house.

All that time he'd spent moaning about having to go on this trip, while for Rhona it had been an escape. Lewis cringed when he thought about it, then cringed some more when he thought of his sulkiness towards his own mum. His mum had needed an escape too, from their dingy little flat, and from him. No wonder she'd fled to that five-star hotel as soon as the chance came. He wondered if she'd enjoyed her course and found himself hoping she'd had the best time ever. She deserved it after everything she'd been through.

He was trying desperately to think of something to say to Rhona that wouldn't sound soppy or patronising when she speared her bacon with her fork so hard that he winced.

"At least normal life will be safer," she said, stuffing bacon into her mouth and chewing. "Last night I didn't think we were going to make it to our twelfth birthday parties."

The moment for soppiness was over. It was probably for the best.

Lewis nodded. "Excellent point. We've survived. And we saved the unicorns. What did you say last night? We're flamin' heroes."

Mr Deacon got to his feet and ran a hand through his wispy hair. His jacket was so rumpled he looked as though he'd slept in it.

"Right guys. We need to make sure nothing is left behind. You're all responsible for your own gear. Go sort yourselves out!"

Mr Deacon: a pure legend. It was hard to get his head round that idea, but he had to admit that the teacher had made a lot more effort to understand what was going on in Rhona's life than he had.

As they dragged their holdalls towards the bus, Miss James rushed around, herding them like a hyperactive sheepdog. Mr Deacon stood at the bottom of the bus steps, looking tired and dishevelled.

As Lewis put his hand out to grab the bar, Mr Deacon spoke. "You've had a time of it, lad. Bet you're sorry you came."

Am I sorry? Do I wish none of this had happened?

Lewis stepped onto the bus, then turned and shook his head.

"It was unforgettable, Mr Deacon. Some of it was hell, but the rest… the rest was magic."

And he headed to the seat Rhona and Derek were keeping for him at the back of the bus.

Unicorns

A group of unicorns is known as a blessing.

There are many ancient Eastern myths about unicorns. The Japanese unicorn, the kirin, is a fierce creature who punishes criminals by piercing them through the heart with its horn. The Chinese unicorn, the qilin, is considered a good omen and never harms other creatures.

In the fifth century BC, the ancient Greek historian Ctesias wrote about white unicorns with multicoloured horns. He thought they were animals from India.

Viking traders used to sell unicorn horns that were really the tusks of narwhals (narwhals are a kind of whale). The traders bought the tusks from the Inuit, then took them south and sold them for vast sums of money.

In the Middle Ages, people believed that unicorn horns could heal wounds and sickness, and neutralise poison. London pharmacies still sold powdered unicorn horn in the mid eighteenth century.

Marco Polo thought he saw a unicorn on his famous travels. He wrote: "A passing ugly beast to look upon and is not in the least that which our stories tell of." He was probably looking at a rhinoceros!

Mary, Queen of Scots brought a piece of unicorn horn with her from France to Scotland when she became queen. She stuck the horn into her food before she ate, because she believed it would show if the meal had been poisoned by her enemies.

In the twelfth century, King William I included the unicorn on the Scottish coat of arms. The unicorn has been a Scottish heraldic symbol ever since. At the end of the twelfth century, King Robert III, grandson of Robert the Bruce, used the unicorn in the royal seal of Scotland.

The Scottish Royal Arms shows two unicorns. When James VI of Scotland became James I of England too, he created a version that swaps one of the Scottish unicorns for an English lion.

For Scottish people the unicorn represents healing, joy and harmony. It is also a symbol of power and strength. But according to folklore, a free unicorn is a dangerous beast. This is why the Scottish heraldic unicorn is in chains.

You can see statues and heraldic images of unicorns all over Scotland, from the fountain in the courtyard at Linlithgow Palace to the mercat (market) crosses in many Scottish towns and cities.

Glossary

a' – all

alkie – alcholic

an' aw – and all

aye – yes

bahookie – bottom

Baltic – very cold

bampot – idiot

belt up – shut up

blethering – talking a lot and not making sense

bloomin' – very

boggin' – disgusting, gross

chapped – knocked

the Clyde – the main river in Glasgow

daft – silly, stupid

a dauner – a walk

deid – dead

dyke – a dry-stone wall

eejit – idiot

flaming – very

gaun yersel' – go for it!

greets – cries

haud on – hold on

haverin' – talking nonsense

heid – head

hen – woman or girl (used as a casual address)

in the scud – in the nude

lad – boy

lassie – girl

loch – lake

lummox – clumsy idiot

mingin' – disgusting, dirty

naw – no

ned – delinquent (offensive)

no' – not

numpty – idiot

piece – sandwich

polis – police

pure mince – garbage, terrible

ragin' – angry

saddo – loser

shoogle – sway, rock back and forth

snarky – sarcastic

spew – vomit

up to high doh – frantically worried

wean – baby

wee – small, and also pee